SINDY

The Letters To The Next Generation

by

Carletta A. Diggs

Order this book online at www.trafford.com
or email orders@trafford.com

Most Trafford titles are also available at major online book retailers.

Printed in the United States of America.

ISBN: 978-1-4269-4486-4 (sc)
ISBN: 978-1-4269-4487-1 (e)

Library of Congress Control Number: 2010914489

*Our mission is to efficiently provide the world's finest, most comprehensive book publishing
service, enabling every author to experience success. To find out how to publish your book,
your way, and have it available worldwide, visit us online at www.trafford.com*

Trafford rev. 09/30/2010

 www.trafford.com

North America & international
toll-free: 1 888 232 4444 (USA & Canada)
phone: 250 383 6864 ♦ fax: 812 355 4082

Table of Contents

To my wonderful mother Eloise, my lovely children,

Javon, Shanale, and my wonderful husband Arthur,

and my precious grandchildren De'ion, Josiah of

whom I am very grateful for having in my life, and who

have brought me great joy and happiness I say thank

you for loving me and encouraging me to go for my

dreams and know that each of you has a legacy to leave

the next generation each of us has a story to tell, and it is our

lives that can make all the difference in the world to those

around us, know that you have been loved more than you ever know

this is the biggest legacy that I can leave you it is the gift of my

unfailing love, may the Joy of the Lord be your strength.

Love Always

Daughter, Mother, Wife, Grandmother C.D

Synopsis:

Sindy is a highly educated woman who lives in Southern New Hampshire. She is a woman who is happily married to her wonderful husband Michael but taunted by her many lost memories of her past, that were never resolved. She is a free spirited woman that loves to try new things and move in various cycles. It is her inward battle to be free from the lustful desires that propels Sindy to step out and move into circles that she would never ever think about. In her attempt to find out who she really is, she goes back home in New Orleans Louisiana to visit her mother Maria, who shows her a chest full of letters written by women in her family who had long pasted away. What the letters revealed was an inward struggle that all the women in her family had in common, a spirit to find love in all the wrong places. In their attempt to find love it cost them years of agony and loss. The curse that lingered on the family bloodline was that all the women would end life alone. Sindy sought to find away to break this generational curse that had gone on much too too long in an effort to more forward. This story focuses on three generations in Sindy's family, Sindy, Maria, and Shania and their struggle to find the true women that God intended them to be. Maria is the grandmother, Sindy is the mother and Shania is the daughter. What transpires is a serious of plots that opens up the lives of three women just trying to find themselves, and live out their dreams without being inhibited by what others think or say about them. Sindy being given bad news that she has a terminal illness Multiple Sclerosis, of which there is no cure feels that she must try to unite the broken ties of the two woman in her life that means the most too her Maria and Shania.. In an effort to do so Sindy writes letters of her own to add to the chest in hopes that the next generation would be spared of the generational curses, and that her present family relationships would be restored.

Family Ties That Bind

"Other things may change us, but we start and end with family."
by Anthony Brandt

It was a great day in Southern New Hampshire. Sindy was on her way out to jog along the lake outside her luxurious penthouse suite. She often used her morning jogs to clear her mind of things, so she could focus on the events of the present day. You see Sindy was a woman of many talents she loved to cook, scrapbook, read and volunteer helping the less fortunate learn to read and write in her community. However her greatest joy was spending time with her family, husband Michael, and her two children Shania, and Mark. Family was everything to her, but the harder she tried to connect with her family the farther she seemed to be growing away from her family. Her husband was always traveling or working that it appeared that their paths just passed long enough, to say what you want for dinner. Her children now teenagers were about doing what teenagers do, which was staying on the phone or hanging out with their friends. It appeared that no one had time to share with the family unless it was during the holidays and even then Sindy felt that she had to make an appointment with everyone just to feel a since of family. You see family ties our what bind family's together right? Or was this just a fantasy that only occurred on television. Sindy could not understand why her friend Lori seemed to be able to connect with her family all year around, and when the holidays came around it was if everyone had not seen it other for years. What makes a family, she pondered on in her mind but as she did it brought up old memories of the past, which still haunted her, like the father she missed so greatly or the brothers and sisters she never had. You see Sindy had a great loss of her father Henry when she was fourteen years old. He died suddenly of a heartache. Plagued by finding her father dead in the bedroom of her family home Sindy was forced to grieve all by herself, as her mother was

1

too grieved stricken to care about anything, except the loss of her friend and love of her life, to care that she had a daughter who was hurting, and who not only lost a father but a mother that day. As she came near the end of her run Sindy with tears streaming down her cheeks cried out "Why can I not have my family back? " As she looked out over the lake she saw the most amazing site, she saw a mother deer and her baby doe. The father was out a little beyond the trees keeping watch over his family. One day he would be there to help show his offspring the way of the wild. For Sindy who would be their for her? As she pondered this in heart she began it climb the stairs to her home and tried to begin her day thinking on more positive things like what would she do in the house today , or what things does she need to do within the community. Just as she opened the door to her penthouse the phone rang it was her mother Maria calling to invite her home for a family reunion in New Orleans Louisiana. When is it? It is going to be in August from 20-27, 2010. So do you think you can attend? Well I have to pass it by my husband but I am sure that he will agree to me coming, as he has a business trip to attend too around that week. "Make sure you bring Shania as I have some things to give to her and some things I need her to help me do." "Okay talk to you later."

Shania comes downstairs as she was on her way out the door to go to school she says "Mom, I am going to stop by Ruby's house to work on some homework and to practice some cheerleading cheers is that ok? "Sure just make sure you are home for dinner around 6pm" "Okay Bye Mom." "Bye I love you," "I love you too."

Sindy gets dressed, and gets in her 2010 Alexis sun roof top and sleek gold and tan exterior car that her husband gave her for her birthday last year and takes of to the community center to help feed the homeless veterans. It is there that Sindy felt a true sense of Family Ties. Here some soldiers had returned from Iraq wounded, physically and emotional by the toils of war. Having been the child of a Vietnam Veteran Sindy could totally relate to the agony of having a father who was struggling to get orientated back into a civilian life after being traumatized by the causalities of war. Not only had some of them come home to no jobs but some of their mates had chosen to move on with other partners. Some had become homeless in the process of trying to find jobs that were none existent. However in the mist of all the agony and pain they were soldiers who had strong family ties that seemed to bind them to their families and keep them and their families strong. The idea of a wife standing by her husband when all his limbs were removed as a result of being blown off by a bomb or a single woman soldier who has to care for her children when one of her arms is gone, or she is suffering from Post Traumatic Syndrome was just some of the unbelievable cases that Sindy witnessed in her weekly encounters with the Veterans. As she went through the various Veteran Wards of the VA Hospital Sindy thanked God that she never had to see her son or husband go off to war. However she felt an emptiness inside that was present that told her though she had a husband that was home every night, he was always too tired to interact with her the way he did when they were dating. The romance that she once experienced seemed to be slipping away. Was it love that she experienced when she met Michael or was it lust? Sindy was struggling with just trying to recapture the feelings she once had for Michael. She was always on her computer doing work. Sindy found that she was establishing family ties with strangers on the internet who she seemed to know better than her own family. She could talk to the individuals she met on the Internet and it was if they had known each other for years. She found herself being drawn to one individual in particular Philip. Philip would write Sindy and they would share all the things that they had in common all except one thing religion. It seemed that Philip did he have a relationship with God because talking about religion seemed be the hardest thing for Sindy to talk to Philip about. The reason it was so hard was because Philip had one secret that he did not want to get out to his family and friends he suffered from a sex addiction to pornography. He and Sindy had engaged in phone sex and internet sex just for fun to ease the voids that each of them was not getting from their significant others. It seemed harmless when they were single but Sindy struggled with it because she knew that fornication was her sin of choice. She had fallen many times before even leaving her own church, later to realize that no one or nothing can take the place of God or should take his place. As time went along she began to realize that these acts were not as fulfilling as actually having someone who would be there with you every day for the rest of your life. However just when she thought she had conquered the demon of "Lust" it seemed to surface even stronger, causing her to think ungodly thoughts and enter into ungodly sins. Sindy decided that she needed to concentrate her energies into going back to school and working on her Doctorate Degree in Education along with becoming a renowned writer. She realized that if she did not channel her energy into a positive endeavor than she would succumb to the burning desires she had from within. The family ties that bind that Sindy often tried to keep alive seemed to be slipping away. Why was it, that all the women in her family got married, divorced, widowed only to be destined to grow old alone? For all the others in her genealogy being alone was not something they struggled with because they had a close family ties that bonded them together, but for Sindy she felt that she wanted to break out of this generational curse that said that it was expected that you will be single and die alone, because you would either be alone, through divorce or through the death of a spouse or the loss of significant family members such as a mother, father, brother or sisters. Sindy was determined to fight the fear that had for so many centuries plagued her family bloodline. She realized that she had to go back to New Orleans to visit her mom and seek to find the answers to some of the family karma that seemed to be hovering over Sindy going further in life. It was for the sake of the generations that followed that Sindy needed to find the answers to those unresolved issues that kept her from being free, so that she could extend the blessing to those left, and so they could go on knowing that all the sins that had plagued the family had been forgiven by God, and thus the sins of the pass could be gone forevermore. That freedom Sindy believed would be the seed that would ensure that real restoration would begin, so the ties that bind the family, could be strengthen within the family, and so that the feelings of hurt that lingered could finally be gone never again to return.

Family Traditions

"Traditions are the guideposts driven deep in our subconscious minds.
The most powerful ones are those we can't even describe. aren't aware of."
by Ellen Goodman

It was a hot August day down in New Orleans, and Maria was just watering her home grown garden and working on picking her ripe tomatoes to work on canning some tomato jelly preserves for the winter. She also was picking some pears, peaches, and walnuts off of the many trees in her orchid when she started thinking about some of the ways that her mother used to can many vegetables and fruit to be prepare for the winter. There were so many family traditions that Maria carried on from her mother and grandmother. Canning was just one of many things that Maria did that was a family tradition. Another that was a family tradition was sewing, quilting, crocheting, knitting, and cooking. You see in Maria's family cooking was an art, all the women in her family knew how to cook, and prided themselves in keeping the family recipes a secret in the family. Maria would record famous family recipes in a cookbook that continued from one generation to another. When a young woman in the family got married a copy of the cookbook was made and given to them in a hope-chest that was filled with all the things that a young bride would need to start a marriage off on the right foot, such as their first china set, glasses, towels, sheets, etc. To Maria and the other women of her family before her, it was important that certain family traditions be carried on from one generation to the next. All the things that the younger generation takes for granted were sacred to the older generation. Since the family always met at the holidays to share in new recipes found and tried and shared Maria looked forward to the family meetings as all the younger women in the family like Sindy, Shania lived at a distance from Maria. Holidays seemed to bring a sense of joy to Maria as she was all alone now that Henry her husband was dead and had been dead for over thirty years. Unlike prior generations before her where there was always someone there to take care of them, Maria was alone in a big mansion, in a state that was notorious for having Hurricanes. As Maria was getting excited about hosting a family reunion at her home, Sindy was preparing for her and Shania to take a long dreaded trip back home. You see there had been a serious of events that had occurred between these three women that caused there to be a bit of tension within the family. Though Maria loved Sindy and Shania she also wanted to be in control of their lives. She was always willing to help but not without conditions. If you did not do what Maria wanted you to do then you were on Maria's bad side and would not get much from Maria in line of financial support or very much of anything else. Her way of getting revenge would be to cut all communication from you and depend on other family members to report on what you were doing. So because of this type of behavior the relationship between Maria was estranged from Sindy and Shania and was very few and far apart. However Sindy loved Maria more than she would ever know but it was the constant feeling of never being able measure up to Maria's expectations that kept Sindy from reaching out to Maria in a way that a daughter should with their mother. The sad thing was that Sindy seemed to have created the same distance between her daughter Shania in that Shania began to rebel and wanted to hang out with friends that were very rebellious in doing drugs, engaging in gangs and even engaging in homosexuality and being lesbians. Shania's attitude began to get more distant and weird by the moment. She even began to become suicidal. Her feelings of not wanting to live began to way heavy upon Sindy. Why would a young woman with so much potential not want to live? Shania was gifted with doing all the gifts that were apart of the family traditions such as painting, cooking and crocheting. They were gifts from God that helped give her comfort when she needed to unwind from the stresses of going to school and just dealing with life. Although Shania was not looking forward to this family reunion she was willing to put her feelings aside to reach out, and mend her broken relationship with her grandmother Maria and her mom Sindy. Although Sindy would rather stay at home rather than deal with her feelings she had toward her mom Maria and her daughter Shania she decided that it was important that she make this trip as she needed to tell her family of her latest diagnose she had just received from her family physician. You see Sindy had been diagnosed with Multiple Sclerosis and did not know how much time she had to live. It was important to her that she made amends to her mother and daughter before she left this earth. She did not know how these two important individuals would take the news but Sindy knew that she could no longer hide this news for long, as she was beginning to lose her mobility as well as her hearing and sight. Sindy's husband Michael had been so supported of her attacks, but she knew it would be just a manner of time that she might not be able to make amends to her family and so she began to think what letters would she write to the next generation to tell them about what pitfalls to avoid in life. She knew that some things they would have to learn on their own, however certain sins especially sexual sins Sindy wanted to help them avoid, as they could be life changing. Revisiting those sins though painful, Sindy knew was necessary to help preserve future generations from the wrath of God and avoid unnecessary sexual transmitted diseases as well as unwanted pregnancies. The fear of future generations of women falling victim to rape, incest, and sexual immorality was so real to Sindy, that it was necessary for her to help those left in her family and for future generations have a letter to refer back to help them see the signs before they put themselves in a position to cause themselves harm.

Sindy had just got in from doing her weekly volunteering at the VA Center. She was feeling so refreshed as she always is when she gave of herself. She looked at the time and it was 4:00 pm and it was time for her to begin cooking dinner, she decided to put some salmon on the grill along with making a salad and some corn and green beans. She also thought about making a cheese cake with strawberries on top as it was her family's favorite. As she was cooking Maria called, and asked if she and Shania were still coming as she was trying to get an account of how many people would be attending the family reunion. Sindy replied yes that she and Shania would be coming that Friday evening August 20th. Along with talking about her day Maria said that she wanted everyone to bring something formal to wear the last day, because after church she was going to have a formal dinner. She requested that all the women wear Red and White as it was her sorority's colors. Sindy said ok, as she had to go and finish cooking dinner as it was almost 5:30.

As Sindy was cooking dinner for her family, she began to sit down at the kitchen table and remise over the various other family traditions such as how when one wanted to date or get married it was a tradition that a guy would get the permission of the family members primarily the father. Since Sindy lost her father at such a young age, when it came to dating Sindy brought her interest to her mother Maria to get the permission.

However with the younger generation they just made their own decisions, not considering how their parents felt. Such was the case with Shania she was going out with a young man by the name of Shawn Jones. It never occurred to her, ever that she should ask her parents permission to even date him. Shawn went to the same High School as Shania. He was a senior where Shania was just a freshman. Shawn was a very handsome young man and a varsity football player for Kennedy High School. Shawn was adored by all the girls in the school and Shania was adored by all the young men in the school. This often caused problems between Shania and Shawn as jealously would surface as girls and guys would say or do things to make both of them think that something was going on when there was nothing actually happening. However Shawn and Shania loved all the attention and it caused them to constantly be in competition for each others affections. Shania was developing feelings for Shawn. Shawn could get Shania to do things that her parents were not aware of such as skip school, smoke cigarettes, drink and smoke marijuana from time to time.

Sindy began to think on times when she was a teenager, and she had an interest in different young men in high school that she knew that Maria would not approve of because they lived in communities that were ghettos, however when Sindy would go to various football games cheerleading she would be exposed to meeting various types of youth due to them being in the same football league. Sindy met this one young man named Sergio. Sergio was this beautiful chocolate looking brother whose skin looked like butter. He dressed in the finest clothes, and seemed to always know the right words to say. Sindy would look for ways for them to meet after school when she had cheerleading practices. Sergio would drive by in his new red Porsche. He would give Sindy rides home before Maria got home from work. This secret affair went on for months until one day Maria came home early and saw Sindy getting out of the car with Sergio, from that point on Maria made sure that she was picking Sindy up from school and monitoring Sindy's phone calls. Sindy was heart broken that she could not see Sergio but she thanked Maria sometime later when Sergio was arrested for possession of Cocaine. It appeared that Sergio had been a big time drug dealer in the 9th Ward in New Orleans and that police had been watching him and preparing to capture him for some time. Sergio was now serving a 20 year sentence in the federal prison. Just then the doorbell rang it was the postman delivering a package; it was the evening gowns that Sindy had ordered online from Macy's Department store. As she opened the package she saw the beautiful red dress she had ordered for herself and thought how beautiful she was going to be wearing the dress. She also looked at the beautiful white gown she had ordered for Shania and she could not help but think about her debutant dress that she wore when she was sixteen years old and about how wonderful it was to have experience being honored for one evening and being made to feel like a queen. She wanted some day to do that for Shania, but for now having Shania look like the princess she was, was the most important thing to Sindy. Sindy could not wait for Shania to come home, so she could show her the new evening gown.

Shania was supposed to be over her friends Ruby's house doing homework, but she was instead out with her boyfriend Shawn. Shawn was of Korean and African American decent. The two had decided to skip school and go to Sea Cove beach and walk along the Pier. You see Shawn had been away from his mother, and was being raised by his Dad. Even though Sindy knew that Shania liked Shawn, she did not know it was serious. Shania had planned in her mind that she was going to be with Shawn for the rest of her life. However Shawn was not on the same page as Shania, he was planning to return back to Los Angeles to reunite with his mother. As Shawn and Shania were on walking along the beach Shawn told Shania his future plan for the summer. Shania was heartbroken and began to run off into the ocean. Shawn was trying to stop her, but Shania was swimming farther and farther out, to the point Shawn could not see her. Shawn screamed for the life guards to help. They came and one called the coast the guards. Shania had managed to swim out to the Bowie and began to hang on as she did not have the energy to swim back to the shoreline. By the time the coast guard got to her she was exhausted and dehydrated. They had to call for an ambulance to take her to the nearest emergency room. Shawn followed and decided that this situation had got way, to out of hand so he decided to called Sindy and let her know where her daughter Shania really was. As he dialed up Sindy's telephone number his stomach began to drop. The phone rang three times, Sindy answered the phone and said "Hello, Hi this is Shawn; "Oh hi Shawn Shania is not home right now Sindy replied". "I know she is with me at Santa Maria Memorial Hospital." "What are you talking about?" We skipped school and came out to the Sea Cove pier , and Shania decided to swim far out into the ocean and well she took in to much salt water and is dehydrated, but she is alright it's just I did not want you to be worried as I know Shania was supposed to be home by 6:00 pm." "I am on my way; let me talk to the doctor's okay just a minute." As Sindy got on the phone with the doctor she made it clear that no one was to be allowed to see Shania until she arrived. As Sindy rushed out of her home and got on the 65 North Freeway, she was driving , thinking what she was going to say to her daughter Shania, does she share with her the stupid things that she did as a teenager or does she lay into and not give her a chance to explain her actions. You see Sindy was no angel as a teenager either, even though she did not skip school she did her share of hanging out with bad kids. One time Sindy was on Merger Island and she did the same thing she swam way out in the ocean, and could not swim back but unlike Shania's reason Sindy swam out that far on a do or dare proposition by one of the teenagers that she was with. Like Shania she could not swim back to shore and had to be rescued by the Coast Guard. As Sindy was pondered what she was going to say to her daughter Shania she saw the exit to go to Santa Maria Memorial. As Sindy arrived at the hospital she parked her car and began to run through the emergency room doors, upon entering through the doors she ran into Shawn. Sindy could not say anything to him at that point all she wanted to do is see her daughter. When she was directed to where Shania was she opened the door to hear her daughter crying and praying to God thanking him for sparing her life. Shania looked up and saw her mother and shouted " Mom I am so sorry, I should have listened to you." All Sindy could do at that point was to grab Shania and hold her in her arms, and reflect how lucky she was to still have her daughter alive. Although she wanted to lay into Shania at that point both she and Shania were too overwhelmed to get into it. However the time would come when Sindy could address what had transpired, and share some of the teenager acts that her and her mother Maria had went as teenagers, and some of the life lessons that were learned from them not obeying their parents. But right now Sindy just rocked her baby Shania to sleep and thanked God herself that he had chose that day to give the gift of life instead of death. You see it was at that point that Sindy began to realize just how important family was too her, and she vowed to let Shania and Mark as well as her husband Michael know how much she loved them for the rest of her life.

Ambitions, Goals, Dreams, and Aspirations

"Do not lose hold of your dreams or aspirations. For if you do,
you may still exist but you have ceased to live."
by Henry David Thoreau

Everyone at some time or another have goals, dreams, and ambitions of which they aspire to achieve. What causes some to go for it all, and others to give up, and just accept what they feel life has given them on their plate? Sindy having brought Shania home from the hospital began to think about how short life is, and began to think about her goals and dreams; it was Sindy's dream to own her own home on acres of land. She always wanted to become a famous writer and contribute to the field of education by starting her own school of higher education. She aspired to help motivate others so that they could achieve dreams. She always knew from the beginning that God had a strong calling on her life. She saw all the trials that had entered into her life as an opportunity to soar to great heights in the world and in God. Just finishing her Masters Degree in Business she sought to start a new business with her husband Michael as a motivational speaker and writer. Michael being a pilot saw himself flying Sindy all over the world to speak. Another one of Sindy's dreams was to travel to the various islands all around the world. Michael had been talking to her about going to the many Caribbean islands such as Puerto Rico, Saint Thomas, and Nassau along with going to Jamaica. She was just waiting for Shania and Mark to get grown which would be in a couple years. At that time Sindy had planned to really get serious about achieving her aspirations and dreams. As she sat down at her dinning room table she began to make a vision board of her dreams as she was in the middle of cutting out things to go on her vision board when her husband Michael came in and said "What are you doing?" Sindy replied "I am composing a vision board of where I see myself in the next five years. " "Can I work on the board with you and add so of my dreams on the board as well?" Sindy said "Yeah I would like your input on what you would like to do in the next five years." This is the first time since Sindy had been married to Michael that she felt they had done anything together that was meaningful that did not get interrupted by work, family, or friends. They knew that they truly loved each other and they wanted to share the love they had with those around them. They knew that together there was nothing that they dreamed that could not be achieved. They wanted to leave something for the generations that followed after them to gleam from. They were working their dreams to build an empire in which the children and grandchildren could carry on and go higher than they did.

Upstairs in her room Shania woke up from her sleep to realize she was back home safe and sound. She remembered the ordeal that she had just been through the day before and thought what I am going to say to my mother Sindy about her behavior. She began to question what goals and dreams and aspirations she saw for her life. Shania always wanted to be a Pediatric nurse and work in the Neonatal ward of the hospital. Shania was very good with young children. She had done her senior project working in the hospital in the maturity ward. She would assist mothers and their babies. Shania loved it so much. Shania also would babysit for friends of her parents while they would go out. She also saw herself owning her own business doing crafts as Shania liked to paint, do pottery and crochet blankets and pillows that she sold on certain occasions like Christmas or Valentines to make money for Christmas shopping. Shania was also good at writing poetry. She had journals where she wrote poems hoping one day to publish them. Like her mother Sindy she had high aspirations for the future. She had just let a man side track her for a minute. She vowed to herself never to let another break her heart again. She got up and went in and took a shower and began to plan what she wanted to do for the day.

Maria was at home setting on her outside porch looking at the beautiful rainbow that was in the sky above, when she thought about what the rainbow meant you see the rainbow meant that God would never destroy the world by a flood again because he had made a covenant with man assuring him that promise. As she pondered on that, she began to think about did she achieve the goals and dreams and aspirations she set for herself. In retrospect she had been a very successful negotiator for the government reaching high status on her job. But she had always wanted to go to law school and become a lawyer. Though she had everything in life she ever wanted, she found herself alone. Life had taken her through many challenges of which she had overcame time and time again. What was it in her that helped her continue in the mist of so much heart break? It was her strong faith in God. Maria had always tried to impart her faith in God to Sindy and Shania and though both Sindy and Shania loved God from time to time they would get off track and follow after their heart and make bad decisions. Maria had a very strong conviction in God and stuck by it no matter who went contrary to it. However there were times in Marias life where she felt short of her own faith. It appeared that Maria expected more from Sindy and Shania than she herself could live up too. But because Maria had her own deep down sins of the past that she had not dealt with her always looked for perfections in her family and others. She found herself trying to relive her life in the lives of her daughter Sindy and granddaughter Shania, but there was one problem Sindy or Shania were not having it. Now Maria began to surround herself by others in her neighborhood and church so she could take her mind off her family. Maria was content without having a man her life as she did not feel she needed companionship. Unfortunately being alone was not what Sindy wanted for her life. You see Sindy had been through an abusive first marriage and was beginning a new life with her second husband. Michael had been an answer to a prayer that Sindy had prayed for, for a long time. He was a godly man who really took his wedding vows seriously. He catered to her consistently and loved her immensely. Sindy could not have asked for a better mate, especially at this point in time when she was going through the most critical health crisis of her life. How was she going to tell the two most important women in her life that she has Multiple Sclerosis. She did not know but she knew that all the dreams and goals that she was planning for a life time might have to happen now. It was those dreams goals and aspirations that were keeping her alive.

It began to rain some more, and Maria was awaken from her daydreaming by the drops of raindrops falling on her head and face. Maria went back inside to continue planning for the family reunion, because she realized that before she knew it the time would be here and everyone would be showing up.

Shania had got out of the shower and decided to put her jogging shorts to take a jog around the lake. She was feeling that she needed to start taking better physical shape of herself if she wanted to fulfill her dream of being a nurse. So she went downstairs to be met by her mom Sindy who had that look like we, need to talk about yesterday. Shania said to her mother " I am going to jog around the lake is that okay." "Sure but when you get back we got to talk about yesterday." " I know mom said Shania."

As the door shut Shania began to jog thinking about what she would say to Sindy her mom about what she had did the day before by ditching school and lying to her mom. Would her mom ever trust her again? She felt so remorseful about what she had done. Sindy her mom had been such a good mom, What she did to warrant this type of deception? Nothing, Sindy had given everything so that Shania could have a good life. Unlike Shania's friends whose parents were still running the streets partying and drinking getting high on all types of drugs primarily Cocaine, Sindy was a nerd compared to some of them. Sindy was too busy going to college to participate in those types of activities. She also loved her children too much to cause them any extra stress than what life had already rendered. You see Sindy already had lived her share of wild living when she was in college in her early years after graduating from high school. Sindy had engaged in drinking alcohol. She used to go and drink and party from Friday through Sunday and then go to college Monday through Friday and party on Friday nights. This continued for almost six months until onto her 21st birthday when she went out and her friends who got her so drunk that she pasted out, and ended up home some how. The joke was on Sindy, all Sindy knew was the next day she woke up to find herself in her bra and panties, scared, she jump up to feel her food about to come up. She ran to the bathroom and threw up several times in the toilet. When she stopped throwing up she was able to go to the kitchen to see her purse and keys on the kitchen table. How had she got home? Better yet who took her clothes off? These were questions she was afraid to find out the answers too. What had been a joke to her friends, Sindy did not find amusing. In fact from that time on Sindy did not go out to party or drink. Sindy saw that as a sign from God telling her that she was following in the footsteps of her dead father who was an alcoholic, something that she had vowed she would never become.

Shania began to approach the front steps toward her home she was determined not to lie to her mom and face whatever punishment Sindy would dish out. As she opened the door she went to the kitchen where her mother Sindy was sitting. Shania sat down at the kitchen table and said "Mom I am so sorry what I did yesterday, there is no excuse I can give you that can excuse what I did yesterday?" "Well Shania, yes I am disappointed in you, but I wish you had been more honest with me about your feelings toward Shawn." "There are some things in life that we do that have consequences some can be fixed and some can not be fixed, you just have to live with them". "Thank God that this one did not turn out with you dying. There are some things in this family I believe are generational curses that have been passed down from one generation to the next. I think it is time that these sins are exposed so those of us who are left can fulfill the purposes that God ordained for our lives from the beginning of time." Only then can we find our true destiny for being here. Shania agreed that she did not want to go into the future making any more mistakes than she had already made. Almost dying in the ocean had made her realize that she needed to listen more to her parents, and focus more on completing her education. After all Shania had so much living to still live for. She wanted a career, to be married, and to eventually start a family. She always said she wanted to have four children, two girls and two boys. She was determined to own her own business and make a name for herself. Today was the beginning of a new tomorrow and Shania was ready to begin living that new tomorrow today. She hugged her mother Sindy and vowed to never pull another stunt like she did today again. It was at that moment that the souls of Sindy and her daughter Shania became at peace and united as one.

Generational Curses

*"The Collective Consequences of a father's sin does not
eliminate the personal responsibility of the children,
grandchildren, and great-grandchildren
by Jochem Douma.*

As Sindy tried to talk to Shania about the generational curses of her
family she began to think of all the decisions that she had made
that might have caused a curse to be placed on the next generation
after her. You see Sindy knew the Bible well enough to know that
we as individuals have the power to pass on blessings or curses to the
next generation. She wandered if Maria had even thought this same
thought herself. Something was going on in Sindy's family and she
was on a search to find the answer so that the curses that seemed to
fall on her family could be reversed. In order to do this she needed to
be honest about her past with her daughter Shania and her daughter
Shania needed to be honest with her. Also Sindy's mother Maria also
would need to be honest about her past so that at least the last three
generations could make amends for the sins of the previous generations
before them. So Sindy began the painful task of opening the past sins
that she knew had an effect on her daughter Shania. As she began
the journey of recalling her past, she asked Shania to sit down on the
recliner as she sat down on the new burgundy leather sectional couch
which was in their newly remodeled den. The den had a big bay window
that overlooked the lake. Sindy asked Shania if she wanted something
to drink but she was not thirsty. So Sindy sat down and began to tell
Shania of some of the things she had done in her life that were not
good and that she felt had made an impact in the lives of her children
Mark, but specifically Shania. However Sindy realized that what she
had thought was something that only had affected her life, had indeed

come back to haunt her through her own daughter. So now was the time for Sindy to face her biggest sins, so she and her daughter Shania could be free of the sins that had permanentated her family for years.

As Sindy began to think about the many sins that had plagued her life and family one that came to her mind was the sin to mess with and seek knowledge from the spiritual world. Sindy's family had individuals that practiced black magic through playing Wigi Boards, voodoo dolls, channeling and consulting psychics. You see Sindy was taught both the Bible and black magic so she thought both were right. She used to go with her mother Maria to seek advice from psychics on what decisions to make about their lives. Most of what they said came true. However Sindy would also go to church faithfully on the weekend and pray to God for advice as well. How can good and evil occupy the same space, they can't. How does one practice black magic that curses individuals instead of blessing them. So as a result the curses meant for others came back on Sindy and her family. You see Sindy, and her family had operated under two different rules that started them on a road of self destruction. When Sindy when reached eighteen years old she went on a spiritual search to see what she really believed of which she experimented with various religions such as new age, Buddhism , Jehovah Witnesses, to find out that their was only one true God Jesus Christ. But in the mist of Sindy trying to find what she believed, she entered into many other sins such as fornication, theft, and lying of which she was not very proud of. She had entered into having affairs with many men looking for love in all the wrong places. It all began when she went away to college. She was studying to be a Pediatric Doctor. She met a young senior named Sergio who was studying pre-med as well. They had met at a Fraternity party. Sindy was attracted to him because he was smart, cute, and sexy. His smile caused her to melt away each time she saw him. In his arms Sindy just seemed to melt away and go to many places in her mind like being stranded with him on a romantic island like Hawaii. Each time they were together it was like being in Heaven here on earth. One night Sindy and Sergio had gone out on a date to a romantic lake and had dinner. Everything seemed so right, and all Sindy knew is that she wanted to be intimate with Sergio. So as Sergio brought Sindy home to her apartment he kissed her and one thing lead to another and before Sindy knew it she was in Sergio arms making love. Sindy was still a virgin and was so afraid of the whole thing about love making. Sergio caressed every part of her body and before Sindy knew it she was intimately connected with Sergio.

Afterwards Sergio held Sindy so close and told her all the things she wanted to here, like he loved her and that they would be with each other forever. But little did Sindy know what would occur was that her and Sergio would continue in sexual encounters on almost a daily occasion leading nowhere, as Sergio was about to go back to Mobile Alabama to go to Medical School. It was the end of the spring semester when Sergio told Sindy he was going back to Mobile Alabama which was his hometown, to finish up his education. He asked Sindy to go with him but Sindy did not want to leave Maria her mom. So Sergio broke up with her, which broke Sindy's heart so Sindy vowed to hurt all the men that would enter into her life from that day forth. Sindy had many men that tried to talk to her but she would only use them, by having them give her money and buy her expensive gifts like fur coats, help her with her apartment rent and buy her expensive clothes. This worked well for her until she met an older man named James who totally turned her world upside down. James gave Sindy all she ever wanted and more. Sindy began to find herself in lust for him. Sindy thought she really loved him because he was so kind and good to her. But Sindy did not realize was that although James was good he had a dark side to his life he was very jealous and controlling. It was not until Sindy married James that she realized that he had a Jackal and Mr. Hyde personality. The marriage started off happy but as Sindy began to branch off and pursue her educational pursuits James began to always accuse Sindy of cheating on him. He did not want Sindy to work or do anything unless he was there. One time he got in a big fight with a grocery clerk who was just commenting how beautiful Sindy was. When Sindy got home James began cussing her out and threatening Sindy that if she ever left him he would kill her. From that point on the dream marriage that Sindy had envisioned became a nightmare. For twenty years Sindy looked for a way out then one day she talked with Maria her mother and the two plotted a way for Sindy to get out of the marriage. What transpired from this action was a lengthy divorce that lasted two years. Once Sindy was free again she still had a restless spirit to be with another man. You see Sindy felt her sense of self worth was in a man. So Sindy went back to going out seeking love in the night clubs. But all Sindy could find is men who were just out for sex and nothing else. Sindy wanted more than that. Sindy no sooner got out one bad relationship then she got in another relationship. This time she got in relationship with a loan officer named Raymond. Raymond was not that attractive but it was his intellect that attracted him to Sindy.

Raymond knew all the right things to say and as usual Sindy began to lust for him. You see the spirit of lust had been apart of Sindy's profile for years. Sindy was not even looking for a relationship when Raymond came into her life she was just lonely. One night Raymond and Sindy went on a date up to some million dollar homes that Raymond had been working on closing up escrow on. and before Sindy knew it she was having sex in the hot tub of one of the homes. Raymond had turned on some Dramatics and Spinners music that put Sindy in the mood. Raymond had done things that Sindy had never had done to her before. Sindy began to fall more into the spirit of fornication. The thing that Sindy said she would never do again she found that she had no control over. She knew it was wrong but the more she tried to resist Raymond the more she wanted him. What was this thing in her that made her a slave? Had others in her family suffered from the same addiction she did? Sindy remembered a time in her childhood where her mother Maria was sleeping with different men of all different colors. Her mother would meet them in night clubs and bring them home to the house and sleep with them while Sindy was asleep. But Sindy was not asleep and even remembers waking up to hearing her mother having sex. When Sindy was nine and began going through puberty she remembers exploring her female body parts and masturbating. At that time she did not really know what she was doing, all Sindy knew was that it felt good. However every time she did it she felt guilty because she later found out in church that it was not godly to do such activities, however she would see Maria doing it sometimes and Sindy would even catch her watching pornography and sucking various men's penises. So Sindy began to want to read more sex literature. Sindy began to want to read various romantic novels. She would fantasize about being with different individuals and being in love. But in reality Sindy had a sex addiction. All these years she had been trying to hide this deep dark secret from herself and her family but now she could no longer hide the secret from herself or her God, because her sexual sins had been past onto her daughter Shania. What Shania did not know was that Sindy had over heard some conversations that she and Shawn had been having along with some letters Shania had writing to Shawn talking about them having sex at Shawn's parent's house. Sindy did not say anything because she was in denial that her daughter Shania would be having sex at an early age. But the reality was that Sindy did not want to see her sin being repeated in her daughter. So in order to save Shania from making the same mistakes in relationships with men, it was important that all that Sindy did in her younger years be revealed. Shania listened, but was overwhelmed as she had always put her mother Sindy on a pedal. Shania failed to realize that Sindy was human like everyone else with desires that needed to be fulfilled. It was in hearing what her mother Sindy had been through that made Shania began to evaluate her own actions and try to see where she should slow down and be a child instead of being grown, and engaging in adult affairs before her time. Life had so much to offer and she wanted it all.

Matriarch Society

*"The grandmother is the matriarch, and by the
end she helps reunite the estranged family."*
by Steve Schrripa

In looking at the definition of what is a matriarch society according to
Zahn (2008) matriarchy is a form of social structure where power is
with the women and with a focus of the mothers of a community. It is
an inheritance in female line; society dominated by women; a line where
females are exalted with wisdom and leadership; a society where a title
often is given to the oldest female of a family and last a society in which
females control the distribution of food, fields and property.

In Sindy's family women had always run things as the men either died
or never stayed around to contribute to the family. It was because of this
type of lifestyle that Sindy had grown up in, that she was comfortable
being in charge of her family. The only difference though was that Sindy
was married and had been married for over two years to her new husband
Michael. The need to be in control was not as important as it had been
for generations prior to her. Their need to be in control was not a wish,
but a necessary to survive. Now Sindy could concentrate on furthering
her dreams while her husband worried about the stresses of life. The only
problem that existed is that Shania was not the daughter of Michael but
of James so the need to have the affection of her biological dad was more
important to Shania than the relationship she had with Michael. Although
Shania loved Michael she still looked to her father for guidance on what
men were looking for in a woman. The only problem though was that
James was still bitter toward Sindy that he did not realize that he was
shutting his daughter Shania out as well. Shania was rebelling toward
Michael out of trying to find love in all the wrong places to take the place
of the love she did not get from her father James. Sindy was trying to break

the cycle of women having to be in control, that's why she remarried to show her daughter that it is possible to find true love if you find the right man. However no matter what Sindy did, Shania had a mind of her own. She was hoping Shania would not make the same mistakes she had made with men.

The day had arrived to go to the family reunion at Maria's house. Sindy was packing her last items in her suitcase. She was very nervous about this trip. You see Sindy and Maria had not really communicated very well after Sindy married Michael. Maria had hoped that Sindy and her would pass their remaining days together traveling around the world. Maria did not like Michael because Sindy had met him on the Internet and Michael had a shady past one of which he was a former Crack addict. Michael had been clean and sober for five years and had become an airplane pilot for United Airlines. His job often took him away a lot but Sindy did not mind as Michael's job allowed them to travel free of charge with the airlines. Michael was originally from Washington D.C. a place that Sindy always wanted to go and visit. Sindy heard Shania calling her to come downstairs as the taxi cab was there to take them to the airport. As she was rushing downstairs she looked at her beautiful home and thanked God for blessing her with a new life, a life that might come to an end quicker than she thought. As her and Shania got into the taxi Sindy thought what was the family reunion going to be like, would her and Maria get into it? Or would Shania and Maria have their differences revisited? Sindy was not sure if she was going to be up to the drama as she still had to think about how she was going to reveal her deep dark secret to everyone. All she knew was that she had a little over five hours to figure it out. She knew that carrying this secret was too much for her to bear anymore. So do or die the truth was going to be out and everyone would just have to deal with it.

As the airplane pilot made the announcement that they were approaching Louis Armstrong New Orleans International Airport Sindy's heart began to drop. The time had indeed come to face her mother Maria once again. Sindy had not been home for decades it seemed. As she looked at her home town it brought back so many good and bad memories. Shania was just a baby when Sindy had left New Orleans. As Sindy and Shania got off the plane and were walking into the airport terminal they heard someone calling their names it was Maria. With her were Sindy's aunts Shirley, Renee, and Lois. It seemed that life was going to be normal today but for how long Sindy was thinking. As Sindy and Shania began to hug everyone outside Maria had hired a limousine to carry everyone back to her house. As the limousine drove through the big gates of the mansion Shania was so amazed by the wealth that her grandmother had accumulated that all she could do was look in awe. She remembered when her grandmother would set her on her lap and talk about a day that she would get the finer things of life and that day had arrived. As the limousine driver brought in everyone's bag Shania ask her grandmother Maria if she could look around the mansion, and of course Maria said "Go ahead." Sindy went upstairs to freshen up after the long trip. As she went to her room she was reminded of the good days growing up in this house. There was a time when people used to come over and play games laugh and have a great time eating and talking and laughing. Sindy sure missed those memories. However after Sindy's father Henry died the house did not seem the same. Now there were maids and butlers serving people whereas before, everyone in the family had specific chores. The house that seemed so cozy at one time seemed not like home anymore. When Sindy looked around all she saw was a house full of women at the family reunion. Where were all the men? There were none because they were gone. It felt weird that there were no men at the reunion. It was a good thing that Michael and Mark did not show up as they would have felt uncomfortable as they would have been the only men there. Something seemed wrong with this picture. As everyone began to engage in conversation Maria had one of the Butlers bring down an old family chest that Maria had been waiting to show everyone. You see this Hope Chest had been in the family for years and was a chest full of letters that had been written by the great women of the family. Unlike most Hope Chests that would be filled with things like dishes, towels, quilts, etc. this chest was just filled with just letters. These letters went back to the early 1900's. As everyone gathered around in the big room Maria began to open the Hope Chest and pull out a letter that had been written by her mother Martha in the letter Martha was talking about how hard her life had been growing up and about the struggle she had raising her children. She talked about the only man she ever loved in her life Sindy's grandfather. You see Sindy never knew that her grandfather used to ride race horses for rich plantation holders. He had died from Pneumonia when Maria was only three years old. Martha never ever really recovered from his death, she had to go on to raise two children by herself. She was a very strong woman who worked hard doing domestic work for rich white people. She used to scrub floors iron and cook for them, yet she never once complained. Martha would walk for miles in the rain or the snow to get to work as she never learned how to drive a car since she knew she would never be able to buy a car for herself. As Maria read the letter tears flowed down from her cheeks as she remembered the struggle Martha had growing up and maintaining a family. It was growing up poor that made Maria realized that she wanted a better life for herself and for her mother. Martha ended the letter saying that out of everything she went through she would not change one thing because it made her a strong woman and it gave her a better appreciation for family. She told the next generation dream big, but never lose sight of putting God first in your life, and next never let a day go by that you do not tell your children how much you love them and spend time with them. Do not let you ambitions get in the way of your relationships with others. We all need people Martha would always say. Maria grabbed another letter from the box and it was a letter written by Maria's great grandmother. It started off Dear children by the time you read this letter I probably will have been long gone, but I wanted to tell you about our Indian culture you see I am full blooded Choctaw Indian. I grew up on an Indian Reservation in Mississippi. I was considered by my tribe to be a medicine woman. Today I probably would be considered to be a midwife as I delivered many of babies and healed individuals with the herbs from the forest. Later in life I wanted to see what was outside of the Indian Reservation so I chose to go to college. It was in College that I met Charles a wonderful Irish man and married him and had my daughter Martha. Martha was the splitting image of Charles she had beautiful red hair and black eyes. The only difference was that Charles had baby blue eyes to die for. Sindy listened and wished she had got those blue eyes genes in her family. She always wanted blue eyes but did not know that her great grandfather had blue eyes. Every black woman dreams of having a baby with nice hair and blue or green eyes. Rose lost her husband shortly after Martha was born due to a farming accident in which Charles had had a heart attack while driving the tractor in the fields. Rose never ever got over her loss either, but continued on eventually living with Martha until she died. Her finally words to the future generation was no matter what you face in life remember that it is your relationship with God and family that will help you get through life's troubles. Seek to sit up a financial empire that can allow you to buy land and build homes on the land and become your own bosses and create jobs that can be passed on from generation to generation. Get an education because education is power. Love God and seek his advice in everything you do and everything that you do will be blessed. Remember love covers up a multitude of sins. Forgive each other, and never let the sun go down on your anger. Stay strong and soar on eagles wings into you destiny. After Maria read the letters there was a silence in the room. Everyone began to ponder over what they had just heard. Sindy said you know, this would be a good time for us to all write our own letters to the next generation to put them in the Hope Chest and once a year we should come together and read would was written so we always remember where we came from, and where we are going. We can also use these letters as a memorial to those who have passed on. So Sindy asked Shania to pass out some paper and envelopes along with some pens. As everyone was writing Sindy said that she had something she needed to tell everyone afterwards. As Sindy began to write her own personal letter she began to think about how she was going to tell her family that she was dying with a terminal illness. What did she want her family to remember about her and want them to strive to complete. As she began her letter she wrote the following:

To my loving family,

It has been a joy watching you my children grow up, and achieve some of the greatest accomplishments. I have always tried to spend quality time with you by reading you bedtime stories, going to your soccer games and little league games. I have enjoyed being a Cub Master in Boys Scouts and a Brownie Scout Leader for Girls Scouts. It gave me great joy to plan your birthday parties. Now you are growing up before my eyes and I question if I was a good mother or not, I want you too know if I was not all you expected of me I am truly sorry but I was only trying to give you the best things in life. To my mother I always strove to do my best to seek your blessing but after awhile I stopped trying, because I realized that nothing I could ever do would ever measure up to your expectations. The higher I soared in educational endeavors the more you expected of me. Now I have come to the end not knowing what tomorrow will bring and I still find myself still trying to measure up to your expectations. To you I say I forgive you for all the days I just wanted to see or hear your voice to comfort my pain physically and emotionally. You always thought I did not need you but I did in more ways than you will ever know. To my loving husband Michael thank you for loving me unconditionally and standing by me through all the storms of life, know that you have been the best thing that ever happened in my life. You not only loved me, but encouraged me to overcome my fears of tomorrow and live life to the fullest today. To all my grandchildren know that I love you all so much. Reach for the stars. Do not be afraid to fall in love or to establish your own businesses. This family has been a family of pioneers always willing to work hard to achieve the better things in life. All my life I have strove to create a business empire that can be passed on from generation to generation, so you could always have a home to come too in the event that you fall upon hard times. I tried to show the right way to live. Although my life has been far from perfect I always wanted you to experience the better things in life. Now I am reaching the end of my time her on earth I leave you the torch to carry on. Remember in all you do never forsake acknowledging God first, in all you do and seek his advice and though you may go through some trials you will make it through because God will always be on your side. Learn to confess your sins quickly and ask for forgiveness. As God's anger will not last always. Do not weep for me, because I am going to a better place, so think big and be of good courage and I will see you in a better place, and know I will love you always.

Signed Sindy

As everyone was finishing up their letters one by one everyone dropped their letters into the Hope Chest. When it came time for Sindy to drop her letter in she said that she had something to tell everyone. As she dropped the letter in the Hope Chest Sindy turned around and said "I have been Ill for sometime and I have Multiple Sclerosis." This disease is incurable." When Sindy finished sharing the news Shania passed out onto the floor and Maria just stood and looked shocked. The rest of the family did not know what to say and began to withdraw to other parts of the room. Sindy went over to her daughter Shania and tried to help bring her back around with smelling salt. All Shania could say is "Why Mom Why not now."

Sindy tried to change the topic by saying "We still have the rest of the week to enjoy each other so let's make the most of it." While Sindy was finishing up her last statement the cook came in, and said dinner was ready to be served. The menu was roast beef, mash potatoes, green beans, salad, rolls, and peach cobbler along with vegetable trays and fruit trays. As everyone was going to eat, the thought that Sindy might not be around weighed heavy on their hearts especially the heart of Maria, because Maria had envisioned her and Sindy growing old together, and traveling the world and even opening a school one day but all that seemed to be gone forever.

It was the evening of the last day of the family reunion and Sindy and Shania were in their beautiful gowns. Everyone looked so radiant and the whole house was decorated with red and white roses. The menu was that of all types of seafood and various salads along with all types of tropical fruits. There was an ice swan that was used to serve punch. The music was a variety of jazz, old school, R& B and some classical music. There was even a room for others to watch their famous cinema movies. As the evening was coming to an end Maria gave each woman a ruby necklace along with a ruby bracket. Each piece of jewelry was surrounded with small diamonds. Maria said that she wanted to show how much she loved everyone and wanted them to know how much their presence meant to her. As everyone bid their farewells Maria called Shania over and gave her keys to a sparkling silver Mercedes convertible. Shania said thank you grandmother, and Sindy just shook her head as Maria had done it again tried to dismiss everything with her money. Sindy was again shut out from being able to do for her own child. Although Sindy had her own financial resources it could in no way compare to her mother Maria's empire. Sindy proceeded to exit out the front door never to ever return to the home of her youth.

Loss of Innocence

"That's what it takes to be a hero, a little gem of innocence inside you that makes you want to believe that there still exists a right and wrong that decency will somehow triumph in the end."
by Lise Hand

Upon Sindy and Shania returning home although Shania was happy to have her new car, Sindy was still a little disappointed that things between her and mother had not improved. There still seemed to be a wall that never could be broken down. Now Sindy decided she must look out for herself and try to create memorial memories with her immediate family which was Michael, Mark and Shania. As she sat at her computer she began to research colleges to go that had a program in Education specially with helping her get her Doctorate in Education or EdD. It had always been Sindy's dream to become a doctor of something. Unlike what she had envisioned becoming a Pediatrician she still would be helping children of the world just in a different capacity. Children are so innocent but some time in life they are treated so unfair. Some children are beaten, neglected, and abused. Such was the case in Sindy's own family past. Though Sindy's past was very painful and sad to revisit in order for Sindy to move on, she needed to move past the hurts she had experienced and hurts that her mother Maria and Shania had experienced in order for them all to be able find a way to forgive their abusers.

The abuse began with Maria, you see when Maria was a child she lived with an aunt and uncle who watched over her while her mother worked out of town. Maria and her brother lived with them for weeks on end sometimes because their mother Martha had to travel with her work families, as they tended to need her while they traveled around the world on business endeavors. However what Martha did not know was that while she was away from her daughter Maria that her brother was raping Maria constantly. Sindy had overheard Maria tell the encounters to her best friend. Maria said that while she would be sleeping that her uncle Ralph would come into her room at night and molest her. She was afraid to tell anyone because she feared she would not have any place to live. This continued off and on for years until Maria went home for good because Martha quit and got another job that let her stay home for good. Still the damage remained locked inside of Maria until this present time. That is why Maria was so protective of Sindy all while she was growing up and was also protective of Shania. Maria would not let her guard down ever again. She was determined that what happened to her, would not happen to her daughter or her granddaughter. But little did Maria know that Sindy had her own loss of innocence story to tell of her own.

Although Maria had protected Sindy as a child, she could not have known that Sindy would be violated as a young woman in another way. You see Sindy was in a very abusive marriage her first marriage in which she was a sex slave. Her ex-husband James was very controlling, and was a sex addict he was addicted to pornography films. He tried to make Sindy do things that he saw in the films. He always wanted Sindy to suck his penis of which Sindy felt very uncomfortable about doing. James would get very angry when Sindy would throw up. James would often want her to dress up like a prostitute and do various sex positions that were not something that a husband should ask his wife to do. Sindy began to hate James and wanted out of the marriage but did not know how to get out. She did not want her mother Maria to know the abuse she suffered because Maria had not wanted Sindy to marry James in the first place. One time James wanted to go home to visit some of his relatives but Sindy did not want to go, so he left for a week. Sindy was never so happy. She began to go out and enjoyed the world a little with some of her girl friends they went to San Francisco for a couple of days and walked on Fisher Man Wharf. They had so much fun Sindy did not want to go home, but she knew she had too, as she had to go back to work. Sindy began to paint and do other crafts she liked like sewing, and Scrap-booking. For once she felt she had time to herself. James was supposed to be coming home on Friday. It was now Friday morning and Sindy was expecting James to come in any minute. As Sindy was putting the Meatloaf in for Friday's night dinner she heard the front shut. It was James, the serenity that Sindy had been experiencing was now all gone. James came over to give

Sindy a kiss but Sindy was not feeling giving him a kiss so James pulled her close and forced a kiss on her anyway. James said "I see some things never change around here", and retreated to the den where he went to the bar and began drinking his favorite drink Vodka and Orange Juice. Before long James was very drunk which was not a good thing for Sindy because when James got drunk he often became very violent, and began breaking things around the house. As Sindy approached the den to tell James dinner was ready James asked Sindy to come over to him as he wanted to talk to her. Sindy said "I have to go back in the kitchen and turn off the stove." James grabbed Sindy and began to try to make love to her, but Sindy said "No leave me alone." James began to tear Sindy's dress and push her onto the couch and raped her. He began to beat her in the face and hold her hands down. After James finished he left Sindy on the floor. As James went through the hallway he heard an explosion in the kitchen, Sindy had been frying some potatoes in a skillet and the skillet had cot on fire. The smoke detectors had gone off all over the house and the flames were going up over the stove. James got a fire extinguisher and put the fire out before it had a chance to burn the house down. Sindy slowly walked to the bathroom and got in the shower to wash off the semen and blood that was running down her legs she hated James all the more never did she envision that he would be raped by her own husband. Who would believe her if she told what had just taken placed? Probably no one after all James was her husband. Later when Sindy came out of the shower James came and tried to apologize for what he had done but all Sindy wanted to do is to go to bed. As time went along, to make matters even worst Sindy found out she was pregnant with James child. What was Sindy going to do now, abort the child or keep it? When Sindy told James she was pregnant all James could say was that the baby could not be his. Sindy had to live with the rape and the shame of her husband accusing her of infidelity. Although Sindy was only nineteen years old she felt her innocence had been stripped from her that day that James raped her. Sindy's life would never be the same ever again. How could she ever tell her daughter Shania that she came as a result of a rape. The two men that Sindy had really loved had hurt her so deeply. How would Sindy ever fall in love again? Only time would tell how the scars of her adulthood could be healed.

Little did Sindy or Maria know that Shania had her own loss of innocence story to tell as well. You see when Sindy was about nine years old her brother Mark had molested her. She had always looked up to her older brother, but one day while she had been listening to her music in her room her brother came in and proceeded to force his self on Shania. Unknowing to Sindy Mark and been molested himself by a young man that he had gone to school with. Both of Sindy's children had been violated , one by a stranger and one by a family member. So what Sindy had heard about molesters often becoming molesters themselves had come true in her family. Sindy often wondered why her daughter hated her brother Mark so much, but she just thought it was sibling rivalry. Since that day Shania became very disobedient and defiant to her parents and anyone in authority. Shania also began to more promiscuous with boys as well. Sindy did not know that her baby had lost her innocence at such a young age. Sindy had no idea that Shania had been throwing up for weeks every morning, was Shania pregnant? If she was pregnant who was the daddy? Shania began to suspect that she was pregnant so she went and got a pregnancy test from the drug store. As she was looking at the results, Shania's worst nightmare had just come true. She was pregnant for sure. Who was the father of her unborn child? Shania did not know as she had been with three guys recently in the past three months, Shawn, Joe, and Daniel. Shania tried to think of how she was going to tell Sindy that she was pregnant. First she had to try and figure out who the father was of her unborn child. In order to do that she was going to wait until she went to Planned Parenthood to see how far along she was in her pregnancy. Shania decided for now, she would keep her secret until next Friday.

Shania was having so much fun driving her new convertible Mercedes to school. Shania was the envy of all her classmates at school. Even though a lot of her friend's parents had bought them new cars none of their cars were as extravagant as Shania's. Shania had decided after school she would go into Planned Parenthood. It was now 3:00 p.m. and Shania was out of class as she got into her car, she began to drive to Planned Parenthood. When she arrived she was surprised to see abortion advocates outside protesting the doctors performing abortions within the building. People jumped in front of her and would not let her go pass. Shania got very angry and said "Let go of me." " I am not here to have an abortion, I am here to get a check up." After she said that the abortion advocates let her into the building. Upon Shania being examined she found she was only a month along. When she found out she knew that the baby's father was Shawn. Shania needed to talk Shawn right away. But how was she going to do that Shawn was on his way down to Los

Angeles, California. Shania was very scared as she knew that she loved Shawn but Shawn had made it very clear at the beach that day that they could not be an item. So why should she even try to notify him. Shania made up in her mind she would raise her baby by herself. Now she had to tell her mother Sindy. What would her grandmother Maria say after all, she had just bought her this new car. But one thing she knew she could not hide this pregnancy forever. As Shania left, she made another appointment for the next month.

Sexual Sins

"Flee from sexual immorality. All other sins a man commits are outside his body, but he who sins sexually sins against his own body."
I Corinthians 6:18 (NIV Bible).

It was now summertime in South Hampton, it was hot and humid. Sindy was just looking at the beautiful flowers in bloom around the lake. She felt so lucky to be alive considering the things she had been through in her past months. Sindy herself had struggled it seemed like all her life with various sexual sins, such as fornication, masturbation, even sexual thoughts. Sindy often why she seemed to want to engage in sexual activity so much. She later realized that she had a form of sex addiction. Why had something that God had given man such a struggle to control outside of marriage? Could it be the inner man that is inherently sinful that struggled against the spirit of God that also resides within a man. Whatever it was Sindy was tired of always feeling guilty and a failure in this area of her life. As she looked how her sexual sins had been passed down to her children she began to feel such like a failure as a parent. Now Shania was six months pregnant with twin girls. Though it was hard for Sindy to digest the news of Shania's pregnancy she was now preparing for the two bundles of joys. Shawn had decided not to return from Los Angeles and had in fact been in the mist of planning for his new marriage to a childhood sweetheart friend. How could Shawn have abandoned Shania when she needed him the most? However as crazy as it was Shania had a very supportive family who were going to be there for her no matter what. You see Shania's family were very wealthy and did not need any hands outs from anyone. Sindy had decided that she and Michael going to buy a piece of land and ten acres of land on the other side of the lake. They had begun to build a tri-level brick home, with a basement where everyone could have a whole floor to themselves that was like having their own apartment. The back yard would be like a park full of picnic tables, barbeque pits, and a playground that her grandchildren could play on. Now that Sindy had become a prominent writer she was earning enough from her royalties to live nice for the rest of her life. Shania had decided to be home schooled and finish up her high school diploma. Shania also began to do her arts and crafts and market them in the downtown mall. Her many painting, ceramics, and crochet items were selling like hot cakes. She had got so many orders that she was hiring individuals to help her ship out her merchandise through mail orders. Michael was still working for the airlines but was thinking about retiring once the twins were born to pursue flying Sindy around on various speaking engagements and traveling the world.

As Shania was going through the baby catalog looking for items for the nursery she decided she was going to make the nursery like a fairytale land with all types of dragons and castles. Since Shania and her family were going to be moving in the next few months into their newly built home Shania could not put anything up until they moved. Shania began to look over the sexual sins she struggled with. She had often times wondered if she was a lesbian or not. Or whether she was bi-sexual. The reason why she questioned her sexuality was because when she was in high school she had many friends that were lesbian or even gay. Her closet friends were experimenting in the lesbian activities. She had a friend Brenda who was the most beautiful girl with long blonde hair and beautiful blue eyes. Because she grew up under strong Christian restrictions and because she had been hurt so much by men decided to become a lesbian. Brenda got exposed to lesbianism when she began to experiment with doing drugs. Here drug of choice was Chrystal Meth, she would get so high that she would stay up all night long and sleep all day long or stay up for days and then crash out and sleep for days. Brenda had found herself in trouble with the law because she began to begin selling the drugs to keep up with her habit. One day she had almost died on Crack Cocaine and had to be rushed to the hospital, from there Brenda was sentenced to jail for six months for possession of Crack. It was while she was in jail that Brenda hooked up with her lesbian lover Gwen who when they got out moved in together and began a life together. Shania later began to hang out with Brenda and Gwen more and as a result Shania's behavior began to change as they would all get high together. Sindy had known that Brenda was a lesbian but she tried not to be to judgmental of Brenda as she was after all supposed to be a Christian and as being Christian she was to love everyone. But what Sindy did not know was that Brenda was giving Shania drugs.

It was not until one day when Sindy had gone into Shania's room to put away some of her clothes that Sindy saw a backpack that was full of letters and a drug pipe. As Sindy began to open up one of the letters she found out that Brenda had written Shania a love letter telling Shania how much she loved her, and wanted her to be her girlfriend. Sindy took the backpack and the drug paraphernalia and disposed of it in the garbage dumpster. Shania never ever asked about the backpack and Sindy never brought it up to her. But at the moment she could no longer be in denial that her daughter Shania had been exposed to Lesbianism.

Maria had just returned from a trip to the Holy Land in Jerusalem. She had gone with her church and was so excited to have been able to see where Jesus walked while he was on this face of the planet. She had heard about her granddaughter's pregnancy while she was away. She was not happy but she like everyone else in the family had come to accept the news and move on. Maria had realized that she had committed some of her own sexual sins along the way. You see while she was married she had committed the sexual sin of adultery with the Cornell at her job. Since her husband had committed adultery before her with a woman on the base Michelle what was ok for him was ok for her. But Maria knew better after all she had been raised under strict religious principles. Maria used to snick out to hotels to meet with the Cornell Nathan. Maria continued in this affair way after her husband Henry's death. Now however that her late husband was death the thrill to cheat was not as exciting. The guilt also began to haunt Maria until she totally brought off the relationship with Nathan. It was hard as they still had to work with each other. Isn't it interesting how individuals can get caught up in sexual sins and make excuses for why it is ok to continue doing the sins even though they know it is wrong. What is more interesting is how the same sins can come up from one generation to another. So you see Maria could not look at her daughter Sindy or Shania with judgmental eyes because then she would be doing what the Pharisees did when they caught the woman in adultery in the Bible and wanted to stone her to death. Jesus turned to them and said "You that have not committed any sins cast the first stone." Everyone left except Jesus because they all had sins of there own that might be exposed. Maria knew that whatever sexual sins had occurred in her family she had to take some responsibility for some of the residue that had twinkled down to the various generations. Sindy too realized that she also had a part to play in decisions that might have caused her daughter Shania to slip and go another direction and now Shania was too going to be held accountable for the actions that she herself had done. The sad thing however was all these women Maria, Sindy and Shania had been robbed of their innocence at such a young age that they turned to looking for ways to overcome their pain. The problem was that instead of turning to people or things to help to kill the pain they should have turned to God. God knew their pain but was just waiting for them to come to him. Now Sindy was fighting for her life because she held on to her pain, Shania was dealing with becoming a young single mom and Maria was dealing with being alone and struggling with losing her eye sight to Glaucoma. What was sad was that Maria might not be able to see her granddaughters, or restore the broken relationships between her daughter and granddaughter. As Maria thought over her life tears began to flow down her face because she had always done everything for her family but it appeared that her family was slipping away day by day.

Sexual sins of Sindy's family had caused all her family to be in bondage to sin, which had caused everyone to be under a generational curse instead of a generational blessing. Even though everyone was progressing alone were they really living? Society had embraced all types of sexual sins as being normal. Molestation was on the rise in the Catholic Church which was supposed to be a Holy Institution. Rape and incest were also on the rise and Homosexuality wars were raging in the higher courts of the land. How could Sindy and her family get back to the moral fibers of which her family had been founded on through constant passing on of Biblical Principles and of which her country had been also founded upon. Where did anyone have the right to put their ideas on others? After all weren't we all given freedom of choice by our creator? Now wrong look right, and right looked wrong Lord help us where are we going?

Sindy needed to search deeper within herself more than before as the demon of lust was beginning to surface more and more in her life as her husband was never home. Sindy began to seek love through another in the form of Internet Love. Because Sindy was so in secure in herself she began to seek to get approval from those interests she had met on the internet. These men still validated that Sindy was beautiful something of which Sindy did not feel as she was very much over weight to the point she could not get in any of her clothes. She lived on the feeling she got from these particular individuals. But they was one individual that Sindy had a spiritual connection with who she had not even met personally, but she felt as if she knew him because of the way he made her feel. He made her feel sexy something that Michael used to do but he was never around. Each day she found herself looking for Philip online to chat and make plans of how to meet. You see talking to Philip was not enough. Sindy wanted to see him and hold him in her arm. Each day they chatted she seemed to get more emotionally tired to Philip. Even though Sindy knew this was adultery Sindy still wanted to be with Philip because Michael was too tired and too reserved to try new sexual things. Philip was not inhibited. Though Sindy tried to get Michael to open up he was often too tired or not interested. Sindy thought that maybe it was because of her weight. Sindy began too seek ways to lose weight so that her husband Michael would be attracted to her again. She even tried throwing up her food, but since Sindy did not like throwing up that did not work, next she tried starving herself that did not work either. So Sindy decided to have surgery as a last chance of getting rid of the extra pounds. While Michael was going to be away Sindy decided she would have the surgery and when Michael came back he would never know. That way if Michael would notice her again she could break off this Internet romance without Michael even knowing. But what Sindy did not know is that you can not play with people's emotions like that. What would happen Sindy had no idea would change her life forever. Life is real, games that you play as a child can not be played as an adult without consequences. As Sindy retreated to her bedroom she began to dream of another who was not her husband. She began to see herself on islands that were only supposed to be places that she and Michael went. Sindy saw herself rich, happy and content but not with the man she had said I Do Too. What was this, that Sindy had let accompany her every waking thought. Sindy drifted further into a deep sleep when the phone ring and it was Philip." I am on my way to see you." "Now yeah so be ready." Sindy's heart dropped Michael was going to be gone but she did not know if she could do this to Michael or her family. But the feelings she had for Philip were so out of control that she could not control the sexual feelings she had inside of her. So as she was talking to Philip he agreed to meet her at the Hilton Hotel at 12:00 noon. Sindy feel asleep and dreamed what their encounter would be like.

Not My Wife

"Four things does a reckless man gain who covets his neighbor's wife. Demerit, an uncomfortable bed, thirdly punishment and lastly hell by Seneca (Roman Philosopher mid 1ˢᵗ AD)

Philip had got up shaved gone down to the barber shop to get a fade hair cut. After all he had to look good for his encountered with Sindy. This had been something that he had wanted for years. Philip and Sindy had been in contact for years never to see each other. Although they had been going on with their normal lives with their significant others they still had this mutual attraction that they did not even know why they were still attracted to each other. It could not be love, because they had never met but they still felt that when they needed to get rid of the days frustrations that they could turn to each other. They could talk about just about everything. Philip had this dark side of his personality that was purely erotica that Sindy was drawn to. Sindy even though she believed in God had an erotica side of her that was dying to come out. She liked to do things for her husband like dance on a pole to act like she was an erotic dancer. Although she would never do that for a living she still was intrigued by the excitement of it all. It was a part of her personality that was dying to be set free. The church had said that the married bed was undefiled but for some reason doing these acts for her husband Michael seemed inhibited because Sindy's husband felt a little uncomfortable with these types of acts because he felt it was causing him to go places spiritually that were not correct in his mind. So Sindy could not share this part of her erotica thoughts with her husband. Unlike James her first husband who was a complete freak, Sindy could not get freaky with Michael because of all the abuse. Could this feeling of erotica have begun because of all the freaky sex acts Sindy had to perform out of compulsion instead of love? Now Sindy was about to find out as she could no longer control this compulsion to be with Philip.

Philip decided that he would be dress comfortable on the airplane. So he decided to put on his red and white Nike jogging suit, along with his Air Jordon tennis shoes. He had one diamond stud earring in his ear. He had a Scorpion tattoo on his right arm. He had a body that any woman would die for because he worked out faithfully everyday. He was a beautiful black African brother. Philip was very successful in the corporate world. He worked as a CEO for famous Music Company called Star Lite Corporations. Part of what had attracted Sindy to Philip was his intelligence. Philip was good at what he did. He helped manage various R & B artists. Because Philip was so attractive he was around many women, but still he was going after Sindy who was forbidden. Philip grew up in Philadelphia and later moved to New York to conduct business. Philip used to tell Sindy all the time that he could get pussy any time that was not what he really wanted from Sindy it was just the challenge and the erotica connection that they had that he longed for. What Philip did not know was that Sindy did not weigh the weight she weigh in her Internet photos she had lost a lot of weight and looked even better than he envisioned. Was Philip going to be for the shock of his life when he saw Sindy for the first time.

Sindy had awoken to her alarm clock, and jumped into the shower to get ready for her exciting day. Sindy had decided that she wanted a new outfit for her meeting with Philip. She went to Macy's and got her a red dress that showed all her new curves she had in her body. She got some new red pump shoes with a rhinestone shoe clip. She had decided to wear her diamond heart necklace and diamond bracelet. Sindy's hair had grown really long and she decided that she would get her hair highlighted Blonde as it would go good with her camel complexion. She went to her beautician and had her hair layered in a sexy hair style that would surely send Philip crazy, when they met. As Sindy began to pack she realized that she needed to hurry up and get to the Hilton so she could get the room ready from when Philip showed up. She needed to order the roses that she was going to use to sprinkle around the room and in the bed. Sindy had to make sure that she had the bottle of champagne ready along with candles to place around the tub so she could set the mood. She had to go to pick a sexy black negligee that did not leave anything to Philips imagination. Philip was supposed to meet her at the hotel in an hour. So as Sindy was leaving her home Michael called to see how Sindy was doing. Sindy said " I am doing great ." " How is everything going for you ?" "Great I should be home in another week. " Sindy was trying to get off the phone as quickly as possible because she had a deadline to meet. Michael told Sindy he loved her but Sindy could not say the same because she knew what she was about to do. I got to go Michael I have to meet with the woman of my sorority today at the County Club to plan our major Christmas party event of the year." Bye for now Michael." " See you soon."

Sindy began to feel bad that she had to lie to Michael but her feelings for Philip were just as real. Could she be in love with two men at the same time? Sindy was about to find out. Sindy got into her car and proceeded to drive to the hotel, and she was driving she began to have sexual feelings tingling throughout her whole body. Her body was longing for Philip would the feelings she was feeling be mutual?

As Sindy arrived at the Hilton Hotel a hotel a Valet male driver took her car to park it in the parking garage. She would be there with Philip for a full three days of heavenly bliss. Sindy could hardly wait to see Philip. It was now 11:50 am ten minutes to meeting the man that could either make her dreams come too or make her life a living hell. Either way Sindy had gone to far now to turn around, after all Philip was on his way now.

Philip had rented a black Porsche to drive for the next couple days to show Sindy around a secret place that he had set up that no one would know where they were. What Sindy did not know was that Philip had some plans of his own. He wanted Sindy completely to his self away from everything that would distract her. Philip also did not want Sindy's husband to know where they were. Philip did not want Sindy to get caught up in having to explain the money for the hotel coming out of her family account. So to avoid all the complications that might accrue as result of this weekend interlude Philip decided to take the full responsibility. Even though Philip was in a relationship of his own he was not married like Sindy.

Sindy was out on the patio of hotel room 255 looking out of the beautiful Atlantic Ocean thinking about making love to Philip when she felt these lips kissing her around her neck. She turned around to see Philip he began to start kissing her in her mouth. Sindy began to melt like butter. Sindy tried to talk but Philip would not let her, when he saw Sindy he was amazed to see she had an hour glass figure. He was even attracted to her even more. Sindy said " Let me put on the Dramatics Greatest Love Hits album." As Philip and Sindy began to dance the feelings became even stronger. Philip carried Sindy to the big round bed that was sprinkled with rose petals and he began to undressed her by taking off her stockings he began kissing her toes, and proceeding up her thighs to they reach her vagina. Philip began to get her ready for what he was getting ready to do. Sindy was gone at this point and began to talk nasty to Philip the way she had done so many times before. As Philip penetrated her vagina Sindy began to scream words of joy and Sindy began to roll on top of Philip and began to take the champagne that was at the end table and pour it over Philip along with some ice. She began to suck up the champagne from Philips chest and proceed down to Philips penis where she had a fruit roll up that was grape flavored. In all Philips freakiness he had never had a woman do this type of sexual act to him. Sindy began to make him Philip go places in his mind that he had never been before. Philip could not contain his self. As Sindy did what she did Philip could do nothing but come all over the place. Sindy began to come up and kiss his lips he was in a state of erotic expression. He held Sindy close and said I can not let you go.

Sindy and Philip went to sleep holding each other. When they woke up it was the next day. They went into the hot sunken tub and bathed each other all over and make love again. Philip said although he had met a lot of women who were freaks they had not met one as freaky as Sindy was. Philip could see why Sindy's name was spilled Sindy instead of Cindy, because she had a dark side of her that was very sinful. However Philip loved ever bit of it. As they got out of the tub Philip told Sindy that he had a surprise for her. Sindy said " What is the surprise." We are not going to stay at this hotel I have rented us a Villa on a private island that I have bought just for us to meet away from everyone. Sindy was so shocked to hear that as she knew she had strong feelings for Philip but she did not know the feeling were mutual.

So Sindy said "Where am I going to put my car.". I have someone to take care of that, you just concentrate on me. So Philip had someone come and move Sindy's car to a place that it would be safe and he paid them to store the car for a couple days.

As Sindy got into Philip's black sports car, Philip began to drive down the Atlantic Coast playing all the famous Oldie but Goodies songs like the Stylistics, the Whispers, etc Sindy was never so happy. As they reach the island paradise Philip took Sindy to a Villa that was full of servants who did everything that she had always wanted. Philip and Sindy had decided to go sail boating and Philip had asked his servants to make them a lunch so they could eat and enjoy each others company. Philip and Sindy could not kept there hands off of each other. What they did not know was that a storm was brooding in the Atlanta. Philip was noticing that the skies were getting dark. He told Sindy that they probably should start heading back. As they were going back they began to notice that the waters were getting harder to control. As the waves came up higher toward the boat Sindy began to become scared. Philip was a little scared himself but he did not want Sindy to know his fear. Although he had been taking sailing lesson this was only his fifth time sailing. It began to start raining very hard it felt like buckets of water were falling upon them. Sindy began to feel the wrath was coming upon them. Philip could not understand the distance that Sindy was feeling toward him. This relationship that Sindy had with him Philip had never experienced in his life. As Sindy began to pour out her heart to God to forgive her of her sin of adultery all Philip could do was watch because for him the days they had spent together was heavenly. As Philip was able to get the boat back to shore Sindy was thankful that God had heard her pray.

Michael had got a call from his boss that he did not have to stay a week longer and that he could go home to his family. Little did he know that Sindy was not home. "Michael tried to call Sindy but she was not answering her phone. This bothered Michael so he called Shania's phone and Shania said that Sindy had taken off for three days with some of her girlfriends. Michael thought that was very weird as Sindy always told him when she was going to be leaving town. Michael took the first flight out to go home. While Michael was on the plane he called a private investigator friend of his to ask him to try to investigate where Sindy was going and with whom. Sam the investigator began to call all the major hotels in the South New Hampshire and found out that Sindy had registered there for one night but checked out the very next day. The hotel attendants said that Sindy had been there with a man named Philip Moore. When Sam did some investigation on who was Philip Moore he found he was a very distinguished CEO. As he called to set up a meeting with Mr. Moore he found that he had went on a business trip to South New Hampshire and would not be back until a couple of days. When Sam visited the Hilton hotel one of the hotel attendants had overheard that Philip and Sindy were going to a private island where Philip rented a private Villa. As Sam did some more investigating he was able to locate the piece of property that Philip rented. As he rented a plane to land on the other side of the island Sam also had a car there to go and get Michael the pictures he needed to prove that Sindy was having an affair.

Michael was now at home thinking did Sindy know of his secret affair that he was having on the Internet as well with a girl named Michelle.

Michelle had been after Michael for years as well. Michael was attracted to her because she had body where Sindy had let herself go. But know Sindy was becoming all that Michael ever wanted in a woman he was trying to think of a way to end the affair but because Michelle made him feel like a young man again he just hung on to her. Now Michael realized that he had pushed Sindy into the arms of another man. Michael still loved Sindy and was not in any position to pass judgment on her but at the same time he was jealous that some other man was messing with his stuff. As Sam called Michael he told Michael he knew where Sindy was and so Michael sought out to go and confront Philip and Sindy face to face.

As Michael went over on a boat to meet Sam he was thinking how was he going to approach Philip so he decided he better take his thirty-eight revolver with him in case their was a problem. Michael could see Sam from a distance and Sam decided he should go with Michael as back up just in case Michael ran into problems.

Mean while it was Sindy's and Philip were talking about what their days together had been like Philip revealed to Sindy that from the beginning time that they met online that he always want to be with her. But he never ever told Sindy how he felt until now. He said that it was all her fault that they had not come together. There had been a time when they did not communicate online because Philip was hurt that Sindy went off and got married to Michael. But after a year of not talking to Sindy Philip needed what only Sindy could only give him intimacy. Now they had reconnected Philip seemed to pour his heart out to Sindy and wanted Sindy to leave Michael and come be with him in New York. Sindy was not ready to give up her family because of someone she had seen on the internet, because Sindy had seen that Philip had been talking to lots of women whom he probably was having Cyber Sex with each day. She did not feel very special to him even though he had brought her over on an island and rent a villa where they could meet regularly. Sindy and Philip played to many games with each other for either one of them to get serious. Philip was now beginning to distance his self from Sindy. Sindy was beginning to feel very used. So Philip now that you had a taste of me does that mean this is all over. Philip could not say how he was feeling because Sindy had did things to him that he could not ever forget, nor did he want to forget. The feeling was mutual on Sindy's part as well. Sindy sought to make love to Philip one last time.

Today was the final day of their romantic weekend get away, as they got their things together to leave Sindy was very sad and did not want to leave and Philip, but Philip had to get back to the big Apple New York City, As Sindy walked out the door there stood Michael. Sindy did not know what to say. Following behind Sindy stood Philip. " Philip this is my husband Michael." Michael was so angry that he pulled out the thirty-eight revolver. He pointed it at Philip and shouted "Not My Wife." Sindy pushed Philip out of the way and ended up getting shot in her arm. Philip ran and held Sindy in his arms and began to shout " Stay with me Sindy , don't die on me. Sindy told Philip that she was falling in love with him. Michael came and pushed Philip off of Sindy. "Sindy I am so sorry, this is my entire fault that you sought to find love outside of our marriage." Michael confessed his own infidelity and asked for Sindy's forgive him for having his secret love affair with Michelle." All Sindy could do is look and Philip and think where do we go from here. Sam called for help and a medical team came and whisked Sindy away on Medical helicopter. What had started out as a weekend of pleasure had turned out to be a weekend of terror. As Philip watched Sindy taken from him he felt a feeling of remorse that he had taken Sindy from the family that she knew. Sindy had not only forsaken her husband, but her God, in search of pure fantasy, but in Sindy's world adultery was not an option it was forbidden. Now Philip knew he could fight for Sindy's love away from Michael but he could not tackle Sindy's relationship with her God.

As Sindy was fighting for her life in the helicopter Michael her husband was by her side. When they got married they had said it was them and God against the world. How had both of them fell so far from grace? How could they ever get back? Sindy and Michael were months away from being grandparents of twin girls. Sindy already had two grandsons by Mark and his Caucasian wife. Sindy's family was already an ethnocentric group made up of different cultures and traditions. Would Sindy be able to see her new granddaughters? Could her marriage ever be restored? Only time would tell.

When Sindy got inside the hospital the doctors had to take her immediately to surgery to remove the bullet. After surgery Sindy recovered very nicely and Michael was trying to talk to Sindy about what had just transpired. Sindy did not want to talk about it at that time, so Michael just let it slide and talked about other topics like their granddaughters that were going to be born soon. All Sindy could think about though was what was Philip thinking now.

Michael was able to take Sindy home a week later, and Michael had to get back to work. As Sindy was able to sit up at her desk she went online to talk to Philip. Philip would click off line or would always become invisible it was if Philip did not wanted to talk to Sindy ever again. How could Philip be so heartless or cruel. Sindy had risk everything for Philip and Philip was acting as if he never knew her. Sindy saw this as a sign that God was causing Philip to leave Sindy alone. As time went along Sindy would see that Philip was online and she would click available but he would not click in to chat. I guess Philip had found someone else's heart to break. Sindy had shared her most intimate secrets with Philip her dreams and now she felt abandoned by the only other man she felt she could ever love again. That day Sindy vowed to try to restore her relationship with Michael and never to look back but look forward to the bright future, she knew was in store for her and Michael as they tried to help their daughter Shania try raise her two beautiful twin girls Ayliah and Mileah who had not been born yet.

Born To Live Not Die

"There are only two ways to live your life.
One is as though nothing is a miracle.
The other is as though everything is a miracle."
by Einstein

Life had been good for Sindy family since the crazy summer that Sindy and Shania experienced almost losing their lives. God had truly been merciful to them. It was nothing that they had done to warrant so much grace. Their actions had condemned them to die instead of live. As Sindy began to work on writing her novel she realized she had so much to be grateful for. Sindy and Michael had managed to get past their acts of infidelity to build a better marriage that could survive the test of time. Sindy and Michael realized that their affairs with these various individuals was not something that was meant to be because after what had transpired each of these parties went on with their lives as if Michael and Sindy had not ever crossed their lives. You see Sindy and Michael had only been Pons in a Chest game. What the Devil had meant for evil God turned it out for their good. Their marriage was even stronger than before.

It was now a new year and Shania had finished High School and had been accepted at Howard University. It was February and the babies were supposed to be born in April. Shania was very tired lately because after all she was carrying two babies instead one. Shania had that pregnancy glow. She looked so beautiful in her maturity clothes. Shania had gone into the doctor's office and had an ultrasound which showed the babies were growing very nicely. Sindy was so excited to see her two granddaughters who they were going to name Aiyliah and Mileah. Michael and Sindy had just moved into their new home and had ordered their white cribs that came with bassinets and cribs could turn into day beds as the girls grew. The sad thing though was Shania was going to have to move to Washington

D.C. to go to Howard University how was Shania going to be able to go to school and watch over her two babies. Shania had to reconsider her plans. She would need the help of both of her parents to raise these two children. So Shania decided to put her college education on hold for now until the twins got a little older. Sindy told Shania that she could use her help in creating illustrations for her books. Sindy was always looking for ways to get her children involved in a home made business. Shania was talented in the Arts. She had the gift to draw. So Shania agreed that she would help her mother Sindy with doing her illustrations for her books.

Shania was getting bigger each day and she began to start not feel well. Sindy began to be concerned so she suggested that Shania go to the hospital just to be checked out. Shania said she would go in the morning and she went upstairs to rest.

In New Orleans Maria were having health issues of her own. Maria had been getting shortness of breath and having hard time breathing she did not want to worry her family so she had just kept it to herself. One day as Maria was working in her famous garden she fell down and had a heart attack. One of her housekeepers saw her fall and called 911. As the paramedics came and carried her off to the nearest hospital. The doctors called Sindy to tell her that her mother had a heart attack and she needed to come right away as they needed to operate. Sindy was so overwhelmed by the news as that is how she had lost her dad. So Sindy immediately called Michael and told she had to go. Shania wanted to go too so here they were going again to see Maria. But this time it was not under the best circumstances.

As they arrived at Mercy Hospital Sindy saw Maria hooked up to heart monitors and machines. Maria was sleeping as the doctor had given her medicine for the pain. The doctor had come and told Sindy that they needed to go in and repair three of Maria's heart values or she would not be here for long. As Sindy and Shania looked at Maria they saw a helpless individual not the rock that they had depended on for so many years. Maria woke up to see Sindy and Shania praying over her. "It is going to be alright, it is not my time to go yet ." They embraced Maria and told that they would be here when she got out of surgery. The surgery team came in and got Maria and whisked her away to the surgery room. Sindy began thinking Maria was born to live not die. Maria had been through so many trials before and had overcome. Having grown up poor and in the south where she was looked upon as less than because she was a strong black woman and because she fell in love with a white man and got married and had Sindy who looked more white than black. She also had a mother who had went through racism too as her mother was Choctaw Indian and her father was Irish. Maria had always worked harder than most just to get at the same level as her other white colleagues in the federal government. But Maria never complained she just went back to college and got not only a Bachelors of Arts Degree in Business as well as a Masters in Social Work. She had proven that if you want something it can be obtained but not without hard work. Maria had proven to herself and the world that she was a survivor. Now as she lay on the operating table her family prayed that they could make amends for all the times that they could not see eye to eye with Maria even when Maria had always had their best interest at heart. Would they both be able to say sorry and thank you or was it too late?

It was now 3:00 pm and Maria was still on the operating table. She had been in surgery for hours but it seemed like days. As they listen to all the code blues in the hospital they were grateful that it was not Maria's call to come home. As they were in the waiting room the doctor came in and said Maria had come through the surgery very well. Sindy and Shania were very relieved to hear the good news. Sindy asked the doctor when she could see her mother. The doctor replied " As soon as she wakes up in the recovery room. " Soon after that the nurses came and got Sindy and Shania and they went in to see Maria. Maria said " See I told you I was not going to die because I born live and not die."

Back at Maria's home Sindy was making preparation to bring Maria home as she needed to get Shania back home as Shania would be giving birth to the twins soon. All the stress of Maria's heart attack had put a strain on the whole family. Sindy had not seen Michael in over two weeks. She missed her husband and her home. After Sindy had made sure that Maria was back home and was way on her way to a full recovery. Sindy and Shania had made their peace with Maria and were now able to go on with their lives that boarded the plane to go back to South Hampton.

Michael was there waiting for his wife and daughter to come home. He had missed them more than they would ever know. Michael kissed Sindy and his daughter Shania and they talked about all the things he had been doing while they were away. Michael had been working on the kid's playground so when the grandchildren came over they would have a place to play without them worry about being abducted or kidnapped as the world had become so dangerous for children. Shania was so happy that Michael had put so much time to doing something so thoughtful for children, that were not even his own. Michael had never ever had children of his own, and when he met Sindy she had already had two children and two grandchildren. Sindy often wondered if Michael had regretted marrying Sindy knowing that Sindy did not want to have any more children. After all Sindy was in her early fifties even though she looked like she was in her late thirties. Michael was cool with Sindy not wanting children as he was in his late fifties his self and had resigned not to have any children even though Michelle had tried to get pregnant by him. Michael always used protection when they had sex. Sindy had known men who she had dated who wanted to have children by her who were in their forties and still had to prove that they had it like that. But Sindy also had used protection as well. That is why Sindy knew Michael was for her and she was for Michael. As Shania sat down she said "Mom and Dad I do not feel good." "What is wrong they said, I do not know," but as Shania stood up her water bag broke this could not be happening it was too early for the twins to be born yet.

Michael picked up Shania and put her in the car along with Maria and they went to the hospital. When they got there the nurses got her up to the maturity ward where a doctor listened to the heart beats of the babies. He said that the heart beats were strong but it appeared that the one of the babies was in distressed and might be in a breech position which was both a risk to the baby and the mother. Sindy could not believe what she was hearing this could not be happening to her baby. Shania had her life ahead of her, Where was Shawn now? So many anger thoughts ran through Sindy's mind. But she had to pull herself together she had to be strong for Shania. What worried Sindy so was that the babies were only eight months old. Having been in the medical field early in her youth Sindy knew that it was easy for babies to survive in the 7th month than in the 8th month. But as Sindy looked at her daughter Shania what she saw was a child, having children. If she could take the labor pains she would be she could not. Having a baby was something that every woman had to do for themselves. It was said that women are the most closest to death at the time they give birth. Shania had two near death experiences to go through. Shania's blood pressure began to rise which caused the doctors to think she might have a disease called preeclampsia , along with one of the babies being breech making the doctors consult as to if they should take the babies by C-Section in order to make sure that Shania as well as the babies did not have to die. Shania was going in an out of unconsciousness as she was in so much pain. Sindy wanted this event to be over as soon as possible because she was afraid of losing her daughter Shania as well as the babies.

The doctor came back and said that Shania was going to have to undergo an emergency C-Section because one of the twins had an umbilical cord wrapped around their neck. Plus Shania's blood pressure was getting to the danger zone. Sindy and Michael were so scared that they were going to lose their little girl. Since the procedure was a Caesarian no one could be in the operating room but the hospital staff. As the doctor's cut Shania's belly the first twin was born Mileah, then the second twin was born Aiyliah. They had to close Shania up but a turn for the worst happen Shania slipped off into a coma from the loss of so much blood. Shania had gone into shock. The twins weighed 3lbs and 4lbs they were taken to the nursery to be put in incubators where they would remain until they at least got to be 6lbs. and their lungs fully developed. Shania was hanging on for dear life. The doctor came out to tell Sindy and Michael that they did not know if Shania would make it because she was in a coma and the possibility of her recovery was very slim. Sindy cried out to the only God that she ever knew please do not take my baby from me. She has two beautiful granddaughters. As Sindy went to see her granddaughters they opened there eyes and they were hazel color and their eyes were oval shaped. They had their father Shawn's Korean eye shape. They were so little but were differently trying to live. You see they were born to live not to die. Now they were spiritually connecting with their mother Shania who was still trying to fight for her life. Shania had escaped death once before when she did not die in the ocean. She had even escaped death when she was experimenting with various drugs and alcohol. But this time Sindy was not so sure that she would bounce back. As Sindy went into the Shania's room she saw her hooked up to the respirator that was keeping her alive and she began to talk to her about the day when she was born and how happy her birth had meant to Sindy and Michael. She talked to her about her beautiful daughters who needed Shania to live so that they could learn how to wonderful little girls and proper young women. As Sindy reached over to kiss her daughter the tears flowed down on Shania's cheek and Shania came too. " Mom where am I?" "Why are you crying.?

Shania had no idea that she had been a coma for two weeks and the babies had grown so big that they were ready to go home. Shania said " Where are my babies?" They are in the nursery. "I want them to bring them to me." The doctor came in and said that he would let Shania see her babies after he had run some more test to see Shania's overall condition. After the routine tests were completed the doctor came in and said to Shania you can see your little angels now. As the nurses rolled in the little cribs on wheels Shania was about to see and hold her twin daughters and began to nurse them. Shania knew at that very moment that she too had been born to live and not die. She had too much to give to the world to leave it right now. God had given her another chance to raise her daughters and she planned to do her best to make sure that they escaped some of the pitfalls she had been through trying to be rebellious teenager. Now she was a parent herself she realized what Sindy had been trying to teach her all along. Today was a new day and Shania planned to spend the rest of her life cherishing the people she loved the most which was Sindy, Maria, Aiyliah, Mileah, and Michael. Shania decided to take each day as though it was her last and to live life to the fullest. She planned to one day finish nursing school and gets married to a wonderful man who could love her and her daughters. But until then Shania planned to just enjoy being a mom.

Redemption

*"Those of us who were brought up as Christians and have lost our faith
have retained the sense of sin without the saving belief of redemption.
This poison our thoughts and so paralyses us in action."*
by Cyril Connolly

In life there are many things that we as individuals do that cause us to feel
unworthy of redemption from the thing or things we have done. However
since we can never be perfect we should just strive to be the best we can
be. It was these very thoughts that Sindy began to ponder upon as she had
lost very close friends to death through cancer. You see it is not until we
have lost something do we really realize what the word redemption really
means. In order to redeem something back someone has to actually have
lost something. In Sindy's, Shania, and Maria's life there had been great
loss of some things. Each of them had loss their innocence, lost love's
and had lost a little bit of themselves to things and others. Now it was
time for each of these women to redeem what had so long ago been taken
from them. How does one go from total desperation, hurt, and pain to
bounce back even stronger; all these woman had heard through the bible
Romans 8:28 "That all things work together for the good for those who
were called unto God's purpose?" But what was my purpose in life was
what Sindy was asking herself? Sindy knew that there more to her life
than just being a mom, wife, and volunteering herself out to war veterans
at the VA grounds. Sindy had fought many battles of her own, such as her
illness with Multiple Sclerosis, trying to work through her infidelity of her
marriage, her unforgiveness toward her mother Maria and friends, and last
forgiveness of herself, for turning her back on her beliefs and foundation
of her faith. For years she found herself in a struggle to have a relationship
with the God that her mother knew. So she went on a search to find what
the true God was, and as a result she found him in a time where she needed

him the most. Sindy no longer had to belittle anyone else for what they believed, because she realized that everyone had a choice like she did to worship whoever they wanted to worship. Sindy was just glad that she was able to at last have peace in this area of her life. With death all around her Sindy sought to make amends to the ones around her that needed her more now than they ever did. Shania coming to near death in trying to bring forth her two twin daughters made Sindy really appreciated that she had been given a second chance to really enjoy her family. Life seemed to take on more meaning now as Sindy could watch her granddaughters grow up so full of life. Sindy enjoyed buying her granddaughters pretty little dresses and hats and baby shoes. Their hair was growing so long and Sindy loved the way Shania could do their hair into so many pretty hair styles, with pretty hair barrettes. Sindy's new home radiated with the joy of new life being on the scene. The twins kept everyone on their toes. Sindy had begun to write books and one of her books was being considered for a TV mini series. Life was good again, and Michael was home more as he had decided to retire from the airlines and fly his new jet that he bought to help him and Sindy work on their new business Air Writers Inc. What once seemed like a dream was now becoming a reality. Michael had become attached to the twins as well to the point he did not want to be away from home anymore. Michael had found the family that he never knew, because he was adopted at birth never to know his biological parents. Although his adoptive parents were like his real parents still the loss of not knowing his biological parents still haunted Michael, but now Michael had been redeemed of all the loss he felt; now he found Sindy and the kids. Even the idea that Michael had not had biological children of his own, did not haunt him anymore either because the twin girls now gave him a chance to experience the part of being a parent to new life; and for that he was truly grateful. Now Michael's life was complete, and his joy of his family was his strength.

Maria as she went about her normal day of just volunteering and working in her Sorority, and enjoying her home began to think about all the things in her life that needed being redeemed, one of which was taking back the family that she felt was slowly slipping away from her. In all her wealth and prestige she still was far removed from her family. Why was that? Maybe because she had such high expectations that no one in her family could live up too. Maybe Maria did not realize that what she was saying to her love ones was really pushing them farther away. All the old traditions that had been passed down like "I am not going to be babysitting your kids," "If you have them you better be willing to take care of them." Seemed not like the Christian thing to say to someone who might have entered into something thinking they could handle their decisions, but realized that after they had jumped into the situation that it was more than they could chew. Aren't we as the older generation, supposed to walk aside the young and be the stable force that helps them learn the proper way to do things, or are we there just to beat them down and make them feel bad about themselves? These were all questions that each generation would have to think about for themselves. Maria had not always done things perfect in her life as well. She at times had been permissive with men and had made a lot of mistakes that she wish she had done different. She too had treaded down the road of adultery herself. Maria knew what it was to be violated at an early age, and always tried to overcompensate her experience with becoming an overachiever. It had worked for awhile while she was in the workforce but now that she was retired, the free time gave way to the old memories of the past coming back up to haunt her, and try to take what good things she had done and make them less validated to the point, it made her feel less than adequate as a person. But deep within Maria always knew she was born to be a natural leader. This was demonstrated through the years in her family. She was the pillar upon which her family thrived. Without Maria's knowledge and wisdom Sindy would have never thought to pursue her education. Maria had always told Sindy that education was power. Sindy had always sought to obtain the finer things in life. Sindy had no problem working hard to get those things either. Her and Michael had been blessed to have a beautiful new home on acres of land that had their own park and lake in the backyard. Michael had been able to finish the playground for the girls. Sindy looked for the day when all her grandchildren could enjoy playing together and swimming and boating on the lake and fishing so that family could draw more closer.

Now Sindy was looking at a way to get Maria closer to her immediate family. But to do that Maria had to be willing to give and take. Maria was set in her ways and was not going to change for anyone. How was Sindy going to overcome that part of Maria's personality? Sindy did not know but all she knew that she was not going to be like Maria an alienate her children from her.

Maria just received a call from her doctor, that she was dying from cancer and did not have much time to live. She had brain cancer. Maria was determined to redeem her family back before she died. Maria called

Sindy and told her that she was coming to visit so that she called see Aiyliah and Mileah. Sindy was happy that Maria was coming to see everyone again. This might be the time to get Maria to see how important family can be in her life. As Sindy talked with Maria she could sense there was something more to the visit than what she was making other than trying to see the twins. But for now Sindy was glad that she was coming out, because it had been three years since she had seen her mother.

Shania was holding one of her twin daughters Mileah, while Aiyliah was sleeping and thinking how she was going to be able to go back to school. She was trying to redeem back the time that had been taking from her to fulfill her dreams of some day getting married, and having her own home, along with getting her nursing degree. Although she had been looking into nursing schools all over she had not decided where she would go. Only time would tell. Right now Shania had been talking to an old high school friend Marcus. They had kept in touch so Marcus had been their to encourage Shania that she could make it through any obstacle. If truth be known Marcus always loved Shania from the beginning of high school, but each was involved in their school agendas to look at each other in such a romantic way. Marcus was now in Medical School at John Hopkins Hospital in Baltimore Maryland. He was in his final year of internship of being a Cardiologist. Marcus had in his mind to ask Shania to marry him once he finished college. Shania did not know that though. But what Shania did realize was that she was finding Marcus more attractive, and saw him as being much more than a friend. They seemed to have so much in common. They liked to go to the same places, loved the medical field, even found that they loved watching movies together. Marcus saw himself owning his own private practice. Sindy saw herself working for a well known hospital, and moving away from her mom and stepfather and living in the quite community of Colorado Springs, Colorado where she could own her own home where she could get a horse and ride through the various mountain terrains and be free to think about what her purpose was for being on this earth.

Marcus was graduating from Medical School in one week. He called to invite Shania to come to his graduation. Shania said she would come. Shania asked Sindy to watch the girls and Sindy agreed to watch them while she went to the graduation. Sindy felt it was important for Shania have a break from her children. Plus Sindy was hoping that Marcus and Shania would hook up. As Shania was preparing to fly to Washington D.C. to meet Marcus at the airport she kissed her babies good-bye and said her farewells to Sindy "See you mom until I get back." "Be safe and have a good time."

Marcus picked Shania at the airport and took her to his penthouse apartment. Shania was so impressed at how Marcus had come up in life. Marcus had ordered some Chinese food for them along with some wine. Shania had not been wined and dined like this since she had been with Shawn and now look Shawn was gone married and Shania was left to raise two children alone. So Shania was very cautious about getting into an affair with another individual. However Marcus was different, he was always so kind and always was trying to encourage Shania. Shania began to find herself falling in love with him, and the feeling was mutual. As Marcus and Shania went out on the balcony and looked at the beautiful moon and stars. Marcus began to share with Sindy how he had loved her since the first time he had laid eyes on her in History class. He knew the hour had come to ask Sindy to marry him. All he had achieved was for this night, so he could complete his life by sharing all his hard labor with Sindy. The only problem was, would Sindy say yes? Marcus was afraid of being rejected by the only woman he would ever love. But do or die the hour had come. "Shania will you marry me?" Sindy did not what to say she was beginning to love Marcus, but was it the lust to be with some one, because she had not been with someone in over a year. Sindy did not know as she paused and thought back what her grandmother Maria said to her once if you are in doubt ask God. In her mind she was asking God what she should say. God said he is the right one Shania just say yes. Shania replied to Marcus "Yes I will marry you." Marcus got down on his knees and gave her an engagement ring that was 3 karat diamond solitaire surrounded by red rubies. It was the most beautiful ring that Shania had ever seen. It was at that moment that Shania felt redeemed of all her past hurts, and trials and pains. She finally had found a man to love her for her. Marcus knew the baggage that she was bringing to the relationship, but he was glad to know that Shania felt the same way about him. Marcus did not know if Shania or family would be ready for a Hispanic man being in their family. What Marcus did not know was that Shania's family had all types of races in it. No one saw color they just saw whatever make the person happy, and that person just treated their family member right then they would be excepted by everyone. After all we all are apart of one race the human race.

Shania could not wait to tell her family she was going to get married to Marcus. When Shania got home Sindy was in the nursery tending to the girls. Mom Marcus asked me to marry him and I said yes. Sindy was so happy. 'Well I guess we have a wedding to plan", replied Sindy. The very next day Shania began planning for the wedding by going out and picking her wedding gown, and deciding what colors she wanted her bridesmaids to wear. She decided to do the colors of the rainbow and have the men wear white tuxedos. Even though the marriage would not be for several months as they wanted to get married in June of 2011. It was decided that they would get married in little church down the street from Sindy's new home. It was a very strong Non-denominational church, where everyone loved everyone. Sindy and Michael had been going there for over three years with their family. So the church members were more than happy to help make Shania's wedding a memorial one. The twins would just be over a year old but Sindy's grandsons could be the ring bears and Marcus's niece could be the flower girl and his sister could be a junior bridesmaid as she had just turned sixteen.

Marcus had decided that he would plan the honeymoon and he would take Shania to the Caribbean Islands for two weeks. He wanted to have Shania's full attention on him. He would take her boating on the ocean, and rent a home in which would be furnished with complete maid service. Shania was in for the treat of her life. Marcus had also scheduled to take Shania on a tour of the island. You see Marcus had a wealthy uncle who owned a home there, and he loved it so much that he had chose not to come back to the United States of America. Marcus wanted Shania to meet him and get a taste of the part of his family that had encouraged Marcus to go to medical school and help fund his college fun. Marcus could not wait to surprise Shania.

The wedding day for Shania had finally arrived. She was very nervous because her dad James was in town to give her away. Shania did not know how her dad and mom were going to get along, since James had to spend prison time for threatening her mom Sindy, when he tried to kill Sindy for leaving him. Sindy had escaped his angry, but not without bearing the scars emotionally on her heart. For years Sindy hated James, but now all was forgiven on her side but James still harbored anger toward Sindy. Now both of them had to put the past behind and support their little girl. Shania was anxious about how her grandmother Maria was going like Marcus. How was Marcus's family going to accept her as well, went through her mind. Maria came in and did the finishing touches on Shania's hair. She looked like a fairytale princess. Shania's dress had rhinestones of every color of the rainbow surrounded by pearls and diamonds at the top of gown. It was a beautiful free flowing dress. The train was very long. Shania had a bouquet that was full of roses of different colors.

As everyone was in place, the wedding music began to play James and Shania came in and Marcus was at the base of the alter. Shania was everything that Marcus had envisioned her to be, she was beautiful her hair was all the way down to her back and she looked like a queen ready to meet her king. As Shania got to the alter Marcus took her hand. The minister proceeded to perform the wedding vows. The twin girls were in their strollers and Marcus had bought them diamond bracelets that he presented to them symbolizing that he would raise them as his own children. Shania could not keep back the tears and Marcus was showing how much he really loved her. After presenting the girls the bracelets Marcus and Shania went up and lighted the Unity Candle showing that the two were becoming one. The minster prayed for their marriage and challenge everyone to help the couple in any way they could, then the minister pronounced them husband and wife. For once Sindy had not compromised her values for anyone. She had not slept with Marcus. She had done it God's way. It was truly at that moment that Sindy felt a since of Redemption for herself as well as her family. Sindy's new name was Smith. Everyone blew bubbles through the sanctuary as they exited the church. The reception would be in the backyard of Sindy's new home.

The back yard of Sindy's house was beautiful decorated with balloons and candle stakes with all different color candles. The cake was a Bible with stairs leading to the top where the bride and grown stood under a rainbow. The menu was a combinations of all different foods like a buffet style, with punch bowls full of punch. Each table had bottles of Apple Cider for toasting the Bride and Groom in their marriage and future.

It was time for the Bride and Groom to do their dance they danced to the song "Three Times A Lady" by the Commodores. As they danced together you could see that they each enjoyed each other so much. Everyone at the wedding seemed to be as happy as they were. Never did Shania think that all her family could be under one roof and not kill each other.

The time had come for Marcus and Shania Smith to leave to go on their honeymoon, as they were leaving in their new BMW to the airport Shania waved good-bye to her family and too the old life that had brought her so much pain, to embrace a life of joy and happiness. Redemption was truly beautiful thing especially when Shania thought she would never be happy again.

Homeward Bound

"Every house where love abides, And friendly is a guests, Is surely home,
and home sweet home, For there the heart can rest."
by Henry Van Dyke

Home felt really empty now, since Shania was gone. Even though Sindy knew that the day would come when her daughter Shania would start a life of her own, it was still hard to let her baby grow up. As Sindy was making up baby bottles for the twins she realized that it had been some time since she had been left alone to watch the girls. Shania had always been around to supervise her own children. Now she was away on her honeymoon Sindy wondered how everything was going for Marcus and Shania.

Shania and Marcus were having the time of their life. The house that Marcus had rented with the servants was more than Shania could of have expected. After a couple of days being completely by themselves, Marcus ventured to take Shania to meet his Uncle Frank. Frank had been on the Island of Saint Thomas for ten years. Outside of the Hurricanes the weather was pretty good. Frank had this big mansion that he lived in basically all alone. It was Frank's dream to have Marcus come and live with him after he finished Medical School. But instead Marcus decided to marry Shania. Frank was not at all thrilled with the prospect of Marcus getting married so quickly after college and to a woman who already had children. He wanted Marcus to wait awhile so that he could get a medical practice started and an own a home of his own. But Marcus did not see his life being alone. He wanted a wife and wanted to have a family of his own. So as a result Frank did not care for Shania very much. This attitude that Frank had became more apparent as Shania was around him. Shania began to feel more and more uncomfortable and wanted to get back to their house that Marcus had rented, so Marcus and Shania returned to the home and went about seeing the sites of the island. It was so beautiful there that Shania thought about her and Marcus moving there to live, but after having such a negative encounter with Marcus's uncle Frank she decided she should remain as close to her family as possible. Shania had been missing her babies too. She had never been more than a day or two without them, so the loss of not being able to see them was getting to her. Marcus was also was also getting island fever, there was just so much you can do on an island, and then you want to get off and go somewhere else. However the water was so beautiful and crystal clear and the sand on the beach was so white that you could not help but want to walk on it. As Shania and Marcus walked on the beach, there was a part of them which wished they could stay, in such a blissful state for the rest of their lives. For once Shania felt love like she had never felt before. Shania and Marcus had so many things in common that they wanted to accomplishment together, but they knew that in a couple days that they needed to return back home, and begin their new life together. Until they could find a place, Sindy and Michael had told them that they could stay with them. As there were at least ten rooms in their new home, there was plenty room for everyone to have their own space and not run into each other. There were four bathrooms, and all the bathrooms came with a shower and tub and toilet. Since the home was a tri-level home each floor had a full kitchen, living room, dinning area, and fireplace. It was like having three separate apartments under one building. Sindy had the home constructed like that, because she always wanted it so if her children needed to come home they could, since economic times were getting harder and harder. There also was enough land on the property that if her family wanted to build their own home they could. The land had ten acres on it. Sindy was always thinking of ways to bring family together. However time would only tell if her vision for her family would actually come true, because everyone might not want to live in South New Hampshire due to the cold winter weather.

It was time to go back home so as Shania and Marcus got on the plane they thought of all the fun that they had on the island. Now they were ready to face whatever life had to give them. Life was so good to them and they could not wait to share their pictures with family. When they got home they would just get their car out from the airport parking lot and take off and go home.

As Marcus and Shania pulled up to the house the gardeners were out cutting the lawn, everything looked so beautiful. Everything was back to normal from two weeks ago when they had their wedding reception on the grounds. Michael came out and helped them with their bags. Shania said "How are my girls." "They are great they are taking a nap replied Michael."

When Shania walked in the doors of the house she could smell fresh chocolate chip cookies. They smelled just as good as they did when she was a child. Sindy was in the kitchen making them for Aiyliah and Mileah so when they woke up they could have some for their snack. Sindy had also made them some macaroni and cheese the twin's favorite dish. Shania knew that her mother Sindy would take care of her girls well and that what was happening; in fact Sindy was spoiling them so much. "Hi mom, how have things been going said Shania." "Fine baby how was the trip." "It was wonderful; we have lots of pictures to show everyone." So Sindy and Shania went up to see the girls, because they had heard through the baby monitor that they both were waking up from their naps. When Shania walked into the room the twins began to cry because they had missed their mom so much and wanted Shania to pick them up. Shania was trying to pick both of the girls up at the same time but it was hard. So Sindy helped get Aiyliah while Shania picked up Mileah. But Aiyliah was not feeling not being held by Shania, so Shania had to sit down on the sofa so Sindy could give Aiyliah to her so she could be comforted. Once she was in her mother's arm Aiyliah was alright. The two seemed to always be in a sibling rivalry for their mother Shania's attention.

Sindy knew that the twins would be in good hands now that Shania was home so she left the room and attend to some of the things she needed to do, for her and Michael's new business. Sindy had to do a speaking engagement in the mountains at a woman's retreat for her church within the next couple weeks. So Sindy has some unfinished business that she needed to attend to before she left. She also needed to plan to take a trip home again to see Maria as she did not sound very good the last couple times she talked to her on the phone.

It was now winter time and the weather man was saying that a terrible storm was heading up the Eastern coastline. Tornados were hitting all around them in various States like South Carolina, Texas, Ohio, even in State of New York. It was raining buckets of water in South New Hampshire, Sindy was listening as the news reporters were warning that tornado Julia was heading there direction. Sindy called everyone in her family together in said "We may need to evacuate to the storm shelter if the tornado touches down. But the biggest worry was the flooding of the lake that sat right on Sindy's property. The sheriffs came knocking on

Sindy's home telling her she and her family needed to evacuate because the water levels of the lake were exceeding beyond safety levels, the levies could not hold much more rain. It had been raining for over two weeks straight. Sindy and Shania and the rest of the family started packing their important papers and clothes, and got ready to leave by order of the Governor of their state. As they loaded up all four of their cars and set on the road to go to Maria's home, as they had no other place to go, and Maria had plenty of land and space in her home. Maria had told them to come home. So as they set to go homeward bound, there was a bit of sadness that they could be losing their home to natural disaster. However Maria and all the other wise women in the family said you can always get material things but you can not always get another life. So as they drove off they did not know if they would ever return back to South New Hampshire or be forever in New Orleans for life. Life had caused Sindy and Shania to go full circle. The one person they thought they would never have to go live with again was the person that they had to swallow their pride and move in with.

Maria was glad to have her family home again. She needed to tell them about her brain cancer. Maria had lost so much weight, would they even recognize her. Maria was beginning to lose her eyesight. She was wondering if she would even recognize her great granddaughters. She needed to share her last waking moments with her family. Sindy could tell that her mother was sick, "Mom what is going on with you." "You look like you have lost so much weight." "Sindy there is something I need to tell you; over six months ago I got diagnosed with brain cancer."

Sindy could not help but weep it seemed that her world was turning upset down. Here she had too leave her only home with her family to come back home and now her mother was dying. Why now just when there seemed to be so much happiness, that sorrow would be lingering over head. Sindy cried and her mother Maria came and held her and said "Don't cry for me I have lived a good life, everything that I have is yours and the children's." Sindy was not trying to exchange her mother's death in exchange for material possessions. For Maria that had always been a tool that she used to threatened everyone into doing what she wanted them to do. So for years Sindy was not expecting anything from her mom, even though Maria thought that was what the entire people wanted from her. Sindy could understand how Maria could feel that as it seemed that she was always bailing everyone out of their troubles all the time. But Sindy just wanted to have a restored relationship with her mother toward the end. As Sindy was crying Shania walked in with the twins and Maria went toward them and hugged them, Shania could tell her mother Sindy had been crying and she asked what the matter was; Sindy replied "Your grandmother is dying with brain cancer. Shania ran out of the room to find Marcus because the news was too much for her to handle at the present time. Shania and her grandmother had been through many trials together. Shania always felt her grandmother Maria never understood her. Shania found Marcus and held onto him for dear life. "My grandmother is dying and there is nothing we can do." Marcus just held Shania and let her cry out her pain. At that moment Marcus did not know what to say. The storm and the death was a lot for one family to endure in one day.

As they all got their composure they all began to look at the news, what they were seeing was that the whole area where they lived in South New Hampshire was under water as the levies had broken and flooded the whole region where they lived. Now what were they going to do as everything they owned was gone?

Time had past, and Maria was not getting any better she was in the final stages of her brain cancer, and now Maria wanted Sindy to call Mark to bring out the two boys Mark Jr. and Joe to visit her as she did not know how much time she had left. She wanted Sindy to go upstairs where the chest was full of the family letters, and pull out her letter that she had written to the family, as it was getting to the point that Maria was not about to live much longer. Maria wanted Sindy to read her final letter to the family, but she did not want the letter to be read until she had died. Sindy knew that Maria always wanted everyone to be in suspense to the last moment. It was if she was just waiting for Mark and the boys come before she left this earth. Mark had called and was coming in later on in the afternoon. Sindy was glad to be able to see her son and the boys but wished that it was under better conditions. Maria had always loved Mark and was hoping that Mark would be able to take over her financial empire. But through a serious of events Maria had felt that known of her family was fit to handle her affairs, so she had put other distant family members in charge of her affairs which for Sindy was good, because she always knew that God had given her the knowledge to be able to establish her own empire, and so she was not really concerned about waiting for Maria to die before she could acquire great wealth or financial security. Sindy had heard Maria say from time to time that everything she had was going to be Sindy's but as time went on Maria also had showed Sindy that she was not welcomed in her home unless it was something she was hosting like the family reunion. So Sindy just stayed away, until Maria wanted her there. It is so strange that now Sindy was in a situation with the loss of her home that Maria would make her home available to not only Sindy, but Shania, Mark and Michael. At times Michael and Mark were not liked by Maria for some reason or another. However now the hour had come for the true heart of Maria to be revealed on her death bed, as the Will would be read soon.

Mark and his two boys arrived. Mark had heard about Sindy and Shania and the rest of the family having to move in with Maria. Now Mark was wandering why Maria had even wanted him and his boys around, as he and Maria had not talked to each other in months. But even though their relationship was estranged Mark did love his grandmother Maria very much. So now Mark came in to see Maria. Maria was weak and was laying down in her big king sized bed. "Grandmother, hello it is Mark and here are Mark Jr. and little Joe." "Come closer little ones" "Grandmas vision is not what it used to be." replied Maria. Maria had wanted to see the boys for years but was unable too because Mark could not bring them to her due to stipulations in the custody court papers that limited Mark for having the boys for more than a couple of days. Because Maria lived at a distance Mark was unable to get the boys so that Maria could see them. In fact Maria had never seen little Joe. Now Maria was not in a position to do a whole lot with them but she was just grateful to see them. As Maria was able to talk to Mark and the boys, Sindy knew it would not be long before Maria would not be able to suspend death. Now Sindy had to pull herself together to be ready to let her mother Maria go.

It was the fourth of July and all Maria's many staff were planning the biggest barbeque of the family's life. Ribs, Chicken, Hot dogs, Hamburgers, and Hot Links were on the agenda to be barbequed by all the men of the family. The side dishes were going to be Potato Salad, Macaroni Salad, Baked Beans, Greens, Vegetable trays, and Watermelon, along with Peach Cobbler and Banana Pie. Maria had requested that a Balloon Jumper be brought in for the children. The pool was ready to swim in, and the whole backyard was decorated with a Hawaiian theme. Maria came out and was sitting in her favorite lounge chair relaxing, she appeared to be in good spirits and not in much pain. As Maria looked out at her family enjoying themselves Maria realized that she had accomplished what she had wanted to do in her life, which was to make sure that everyone in her family had a decent way of living. Everyone in her family were doing well in their educational endeavors, Sindy was about to get her Doctorate in Education, Mark was in Culinary School, Shania was excepted to go to Nursing School and Marcus was about to become a surgeon at John Hopkins Hospital in the Cardiology department of the hospital doing heart surgery. So Maria was just enjoying her rest of her life to the fullest, and loving that for once in her life she was not totally alone.

The Final Departure

"Change is certain. Peace is followed by disturbances;
departure of evil men by their return.
Such reoccurrence should constitute occasions for sadness but
realities for awareness, so that one may be happy in the interim."
by Percy Bysshe Shelley

The phone rang it was for Sindy the insurance adjustor had called to tell Sindy about all the damage that had been caused by the winter storm that had devastated Sindy's dream home. The whole home was totally destroyed so the insurance adjuster needed to know if Sindy and Michael wanted to have their home rebuilt, or just settle for the money in order to rebuild somewhere else. Sindy told the insurance adjustor that they would have to get back to him, because at that point she did not know what her family wanted her to do. After all Maria was not getting any better in fact the doctors were giving the family a matter of days before Maria would be gone. In fact the doctors had asked that the family assemble in the morning so that could administer the last does of Morphine so Maria could go to sleep without any pain. This was hard for Sindy to do, but the cancer had hit all Maria's vital organs and she was going to go anyway. So as Sindy kissed her mother she left Maria and went to bed as the next day was not going to be a good day.

Morning time had come. Sindy was assembling all the family members together in Maria's bedroom. Maria's family doctor Johnson was present to administer the final dose of Morphine into Maria's arm. But before Maria went unconscious, she requested that each family member present come forward so she could say her final farewells as they knew that Maria was going home to be with the Lord. As Doctor Johnson began to administer the final dose of medicine Maria began to drift into a deep sleep and then she breathed her last breath. As everyone cried and tried to get themselves together. Sindy said there was one last request that Maria had requested of her as her daughter to do and that was to read her final letter to the next generation. The letter read as the following:

Dear Family:

Do not weep for me. I have lived a great life. Even though it has not been without its share of pain, having had the opportunity to have had a great family has been the best part of this journey. I know that all of you have not really understood why I did the things I did sometimes, but it was always with your best interest in mind. To my daughter Sindy I know you always thought I never loved you, because it seemed like I never liked any of your choices you made in husbands, but it was only because I knew you could have chosen the cream of the top as far as professional men. Michael I must admit I did not like you, because of your shady past but I realized as time went on that you were a blessing to my daughter as you stood by her through her illness and her many surgeries. To my granddaughter Shania I know that you felt that I did not like you very much because of the many mistakes you made in your youth, but I never blamed you because you were not probably guided by your parents. You were always the apple of my eye. I hated that you had to have your daughters without their father but I see how great a mother you have been to your beautiful twin daughters. You have made me the happiest grandmother, in just the way you were able to go through the various trials and still be able to go after you dream to become a nurse. To Mark I know that you did not understand when you were young, that I was hard on you but it was because I was grooming you to be the man to take over this family. Up to this point there had only been woman running the family, not by choice but by destiny. But it appeared that through your mother Sindy that a new generation of men would be born that could step up to the plate and run the family, like the way God had destined it to be. So if I was hard on you please forgive me. To my great grandchildren know that you can do anything in life that you chose too. Know that I wish I could be with you, but fate did not allow me to be with you. Hopefully you get everything that you ever want from life. Life is hard but it can be sweet if you remember to always think about others more than yourself.

Look to God to guide your steps and you will never fail. I love you all forever, and wish you peace and happiness.

Love Always Maria

Now that Maria had past, there was the planning of the funeral that needed to be done. Maria had actually written in her Will how she wanted her final departure to be carried out. Now the day had arrived for the reading of the Maria's Will. The reading of the Will was not something that Sindy wanted to hear, so she withdrew herself from the room. She had already told Maria's lawyer that whatever was in the Will for her to just have it delivered to her. So as everyone sat down. Maria had Willed her car to her great nephew. Maria had her furniture Willed to her best friend Sandy. Her full Mink Coat she gave to her granddaughter Shania. The mansion she gave to her grandson Mark. To her four great grandchildren she had educational funds set up for each of them to go to college of over $150,000 dollars. For Sindy Maria left all the other financial assets including jewelry, monetary values, as long as painting etc. What was amazing that all the people that Maria had involved in her affairs before her death she took out of the Will at the end.

Maria was buried where her mother was buried in Walnut Arkansas. Now that all Maria's affairs were settled Sindy and the rest of the family needed to decide what they were going to do with the rest of their lives. Shania decided to move to Baltimore Maryland. so that her and Marcus could be close to their work at John Hopkins Hospital where Marcus would be able to establish his own private practice as well and be able to participate in private heart research. Marcus had found a beautiful Penthouse that was five bedrooms where the twins could have separate rooms of their own, and one extra room for Shania to have one more child by Marcus and then they could have their own Master Bedroom fully loaded with a fireplace and a sitting room and matching double sinks in the bathroom. The bathroom was to die for, as it had a glass shower and sunken tub full with power jets to ease all ones soar muscles. Shania and Michael were preparing to leave, so that they could get started on buying new furniture for their new home.

Mark decided that he needed to go home and pack and more into his new mansion that Maria had given him. Mark's life had changed overnight and him and his boys were going to know what it meant to live the life of the rich and famous. Mark was going to sell everything he had, and start off fresh in his new surroundings. Mark had decided to open a Creole Restaurant where he would serve some of the favorite Louisiana cuisines. Like seafood dishes like Gumbo, Fried Chicken. and Dirty Rice among other dishes that Maria had taught him to make. Mark planned to have the staff who had been so loyal to Maria remain if they chose too. Mark was also planning to ask Michaela a girl he had been dating for over two years to marry him. Mark planned to do that before he left Los Angeles. Michaela was an Executive Secretary for Apple Computers. Mark was not sure how all this was going to work out or even if Michaela would say yes. Mark was going to ask Michaela at dinner on the Queen Mary a ship was known for their seafood menu. Mark had to pick up the engagement ring and get dressed.

As Mark went to pick Michaela at her townhouse apartment in Hollywood California he rang the doorbell and Michaela was looking gorgeous as usual in her purple dress trimmed in gold beads. She had on high purple pumps. She had on Mark's favorite perfume Black Diamond by Elizabeth Taylor. As they got in the car to go to Long Beach Harbor Mark was praying that Michaela would say yes to his proposal. When they arrived at the Pier Mark did the gentlemen thing and opened Michaela's door. While they were eating Mark told Michaela about all that had happened with his grandmother Maria. He told her that Maria had given him her mansion. Michaela said to Mark "So does this mean that you are going to be moving," "Yes but I was hoping you would go with me." "What are you saying Marcus, " replied Michaela. "Will you marry me Michaela." "After a long pause Michaela said "Yes Mark I will marry you." Mark sealed the deal with a kiss. So Mark was about to make a final departure from the only life he had known, as a young adult to move to another area that he had left so many years ago. But at least he would not be going home alone. he would have a new wife along with his boys to start a new beginning with.

Sindy and Michael had decided that they did not want to move back to South New Hampshire, but wanted to move to Santa Barbara California to enjoy the beauty of the weather as well as the beaches. They decided they would let their kids live their lives as they lived their life. Instead of building another home they decided to downsize to a newly built condominium that had just been built in the hills. Every room of their home had a view that overlooked the ocean. Their home had only four bedrooms that consisted of two rooms, a Master Bedroom, guest room, an office and a movie room full of all types of audiovisual equipment, and a Big Screen Sony Bravia.

Michael was in seventh heaven and Sindy was happy that now all that they had to concern themselves with was with themselves. They were beginning to travel all over the world. They had just got back from a trip to Ireland. They invested in Time Shares that were all over the world, so that they could go and stay in whenever they traveled. Michael could rent planes to fly anywhere they wanted so they did not have to use the commercial airlines anymore. In fact Michael had just decided to buy a Lear Jet for the family own business Air Writers Inc. So life was doing good, so as Sindy and Michael made their final departure from the famous family mansion of her mother Maria Sindy was not sad at all, but glad that in the end that Maria was able to make peace with her family and that the rest of the family was able to make peace with each other as well.

Maria had been dead for fifteen years and Mark's older son Mark Jr. had just graduated from Southern University and had got drafted to play football for the San Francisco 49ers. Mark Jr. was so happy to be leaving New Orleans. He always thought of the day he would go to California and met a Cali Girl. For his whole life he only known the life that his grandmothers knew here in New Orleans, now he wanted to find out what things life had for him to experience. He had listen to Maria's advise that education was power. He listened to Sindy that encourage him to try new things so she paid for Marcus Jr. to have piano lessons, drum lessons and along with paying for all his football league uniforms and events. This had paid off in the long run because now Mark Jr. was going to play in the NFL. Maria had made sure that none of her great grandchildren had to worry about paying for college. If Maria could see Mark Jr. now, she would be so proud.. Sindy was so proud of her grandson and was even more happy that he played for her favorite team the San Francisco 49ers. She was also glad that he would be close so she could see him often. The good news was that Sindy had just recently found out that her disease Multiple Sclerosis had gone in permanent remission because she had not had an attack in five years. Because Sindy was happy mentally it has caused her physically condition to be healed. Now as Sindy waited for Mark Jr. to make his final departure to come to California Sindy planned to go to Baltimore Maryland to help plan the twin girls Debut as Debutantes for Maria's Sorority. Now Aiyliah and Mileah were sixteen and were being introduced to society. Boy had time come full circle as Sindy was once a Debutante for the same Sorority so many years before. Maria continues to live on in the lives of her family, and Sindy and Shania continue to carry on the family trilogy.

References

Brandt, A. (2009). *Family Traditions Ideas Celebrating Old and New Family Traditions.* http://www.all-famous-quotes.com/family-quotes.html

Connolly, C. (2010). *Redemption Quotes.* http://think.exist.com/quotes/with/keyword/redemption/html

Douma, J. (2007). *The Sins of the Father's Quotes.* http://www/RayFowler.org

Dyke, H., V., (2010). *Quotations About Home.* http://www.quotesgarden.com/home.html

Einstein, (2010). *Spiritual Quotes on Living & Dying.* http://www.oprah.com/community/thread/103076

Goodman, E. (2010). *Brainy Quote Ellen Goodman Quotes.* http://www.brainyquote.com/quotes/quotes/e/ellengoodman/22226.html

Hand, L. (2010). *Loss of Innocence Lise Hand Quotes.* http://thinkexist.com/quotes/Lise-Hand/

Schirripa, S. (2010). *Random Quotes.* http://www.famousqoutes.com/quotation/thegrandmother-is-the-matriarch-and-by-the-end-she-helps-reunite-the-estranged-family

Seneca, Roman Philosopher, (2010). *Adultery Quotes.* http://think.exist.com/quotations/adultery

Shelley, P., B. (2010). *Departure Quotes.* http://www.brainyquotes.com/quotes/keywords/departure.html

Thoreau, H., D. (2010). *Dream, Plans, Goals Quotes.*
    http://www.bellaonline.com/articles/art.17573.asp.

Zhan, K. (2008). *Matriarch.*
    http://www.matriarch-society.com

Zondervan, (2005). *New International Bible (NIV), Life Application
    Study Bible.* Grand Rapids, Michigan: Tyndale House Publishers,
    Inc.